I'm Drinking From My Saucer

'Cause My Cup Overflows

I'm Drinking From My Saucer

'Cause My Cup Overflows

by Carl A. Otto

Copyright 2007 by Carl A. Otto
Printed in the United States

All rights reserved by author

ISBN 978-1-58597-447-4
Library of Congress Control Number: 2007934190

4500 College Boulevard
Overland Park, Kansas 6621
888-888-7696
www.leatherspublishing.com

DEDICATION:

This book is dedicated to Kathy Roney, owner and operator of the Iola Tea and Coffee Shoppe in Iola, Kansas. She has been an inspiration to me in her dogged persistence, against many odds, to establish her unique business, and in her promotion of my writings at her shoppe, not only by actual sales, but also by holding book signings for me. Her efforts have not gone unnoticed.

FOREWORD

This book is a collection of short stories; some are lengthy enough to have been stretched into a full length novel, but I am of the opinion that the value of a story need not be determined by the number of words it contains. I suppose, in my lifetime, I could count the total times on my fingers at which I sat down with a book and read it from cover to cover without stopping. I guess I need more exercises in patience. And, I honestly feel that most novels could have been written using of half the words.

Most of the stories herein are love stories and a few of them might even reveal an incident that I personally experienced, or that someone experienced who is close to me. Nearly all the names are fictional "to protect the innocent," as the old saying goes.

You will not find descriptions of steamy sex scenes in my stories, nor will you find vulgar language. I am appalled at the language used in so many of our books, our movies and TV programs. It is not that I have not "heard it all." I am an Army veteran who can, if I chose to do so, stand toe to toe, nose to nose with anyone and use language that would put a pirate to shame; however, I chose not to do so. I realize, that in writing, there are many times when coarse language might even be needed for intended affect, as long as the name of the Lord is not violated; I have used some in

vii

previous writings, but I have decided to avoid language that might be the least bit offensive to any and all who read this book.

Carl A. Otto

ABOUT THE AUTHOR

Carl Alonzo Otto was born February 12, 1926 in Pierce, Nebraska, the second child of Clyde and Myrtle and a member of a loving family. He had one sister and four brothers as well as a large extended family. From the time he was able to walk, he was a venturesome, reckless, curious, fearless kind of individual. Throughout his childhood, youth, early adulthood, and even a few times as an old geezer, he has repeatedly placed himself in positions and situations in which his actual life was in danger. He was also an extremely lucky person, because he was able to emerge unscathed from the vast majority of his "close encounters."

This man is no cat, because it is said that a cat has nine lives; he most certainly must have had, and still has some stored up, many more than nine. He has survived, several early childhood scrapes, was revived from a drowning, a fall on his back from a second story window, a critical head injury as a farmhand, three automobile wrecks and one motorcycle wreck, ninety-six days in a combat zone during WWII, a major crunch under a falling tree, major colon surgery and a heart attack at age eighty one; to name a few.

He was married to Aletha Faye McCants for nearly fifty-four years before he lost her in 2001. They had two sons. William "Bill" Clyde Otto is a retired educator who is now a Kansas State Representative and Kenneth "Yogi" Porter

Otto who is an Elementary Principal. He is the grandfather of six beautiful granddaughters and seven handsome grandsons and grandsons-in-law. He is a great grandfather of three girls and three boys, and he is the proud father-in-law of the wives of his sons.

Tragically he lost one daughter-in-law and her infant son, Debrah Jeanne Wilson Otto and little Carl William to unexpected, but natural causes.

Otto is a high school dropout who ended a thirty-eight year career as a teacher, athletic coach, principal and superintendent of schools. He is a very fortunate individual with many God-given talents for which he is truly grateful. Indeed his cup runneth over.

Carl A. Otto
1804 N Locust
Pittsburg, Kansas 66762

Phone 620 235-0364
Cell   620 724-2084
fatkrout@hotmail.com

TABLE OF CONTENTS:

Dedication v

Foreword.. vii

About the Author ix

My Cup Runneth Over 1

My Peaceful Sunday 3

Wet Pants.. 41

Grandpa Bern's Hotel... 51

He Was There 79

Whatever Happened to Elmer....................................... 125

Is it Really You 143

Kid Power 163

Congo and Samantha.. 187

Uncle Charlie is a Rounder 211

Cherokee Wisdom... 243

Lost Behind Enemy Lines.. 249

Epilogue 293

MY CUP OVERFLOWS

By

Michael Combs

I never made a fortune, and it's probably too late now,
But I don't worry about it much, I'm happy anyhow.
And as I go along life's way, I'm reaping better than I sowed.
I'm drinking from my saucer, 'cause my cup is overflowed.

I haven't got a lot of riches, and sometimes the goin is tough
But I've got loving ones all around me, and that makes me rich enough.
I thank God for all His blessings, and the mercies He's bestowed.
I'm drinkin from my saucer, 'cause my cup is overflowed.

I remember times when things went wrong. My faith wore somewhat thin
But all at once the dark clouds broke, and the sun peeped through again.
So, Lord help me not to gripe 'bout the tough rows I have hoed.
I'm drinkin from my saucer, 'cause my cup is overflowed.

If God gives me strength and courage, when the way grows steep and rough,
I'll not ask for other blessings, I'm already blessed enough.

Carl Otto

And may I never be too busy to help others bear their loads
Then I'll keep on drinkin from my saucer, 'cause my cup is overflowed.

(Last verse by Carl Otto)
When I think of how many people in this world who have it
worse
I realize how blessed we all are as I contemplate this verse.
We should all resolve to be positive as we travel down our roads
'Cause we're all drinkin from our saucers. Our cups are over-
flowed.

MY PEACEFUL
SUNDAY

MY PEACEFUL SUNDAY

Ben Wright had just finished putting his tools away and was headed for the time clock to punch out; it was 5:22 p.m. on Saturday afternoon and he was looking forward to a pleasant Saturday evening and peaceful Sunday with his family. They had no particular plans; other than their regular 10:00 Sunday School and Church Service; however, the weather was supposed to be great for an early spring day, so he had been thinking about taking Sue and the kids for a drive and eating lunch somewhere different.

"Hey Ben," He heard coming from the foreman's office. "Could you hold up a minute? I need to ask you something."

"No Problem, Frank. You want me to come in there?"

"Yeah, come on in if you don't mind."

He walked over to the foreman's office and leaned on the door jam. Frank was talking on the telephone, so Ben just stood there while he finished the conversation. Frank placed his hand over the telephone receiver and turned.

"Ben, this is some big wheel from Franklin Tool Co., and, he wants to know if there is any way he could pick up his order tonight."

Carl Otto

Ben answered, "That Franklin Tool order is several hours from being complete. I wasn't figuring on getting it finished and packed before Monday morning."

"He said if we would get it ready, he would send someone here from Springfield to pick it up. Could you stay and help me finish getting it ready? I will wait for his pick-up man."

"Sure, I'll stay; but I need to give Sue a call and tell her I will be late."

Frank turned back to his conversation, "Send your man. We should have it ready by the time he gets here."

He hung up the telephone and Ben picked it up to dial his home number.

"Hi sweetie pie, is Momma there? I need to talk to her."

His little daughter asked, "Daddy, where are you?"

"I'm still at work Sugar. Tell Momma I need to talk to her."

"Ain't you coming home?"

"Cora, Honey, of course I'm coming home, but I need to tell Momma I will be a little late. Okay? Now go tell her to come to the phone."

"Okay Daddy."

After a short pause, he hears, "Hello Ben, what's up?"

"Could you and the kids go ahead and eat supper? I am going to be delayed for a while. Frank wants me to stay and help finish a hurry-up order that needs to be picked up tonight."

My Peaceful Sunday

"How long do you think it will take?"

"I don't really know, but I would guess at least a couple of hours; possibly more"

"Okay Honey, I'll keep something back for you. I can warm it up when you get here. You give me a call when you leave there."

"You're a doll, I love you; see you later."

He turned to Frank and said, "Okay Buddy, let's get cracking."

At the same time, ninety-five miles north of Ben's place, in a different setting, another telephone conversation was developing. A young woman was reaching for a phone and saying to her two children, "He has finally passed out. Go get your things while I call Johnnie."

She picked up the phone and dialed a number.

"Bring it over Johnnie. We are ready to leave right now."

She put the phone back on the cradle and went to a closet where she retrieved a large suitcase and a laundry bag. By the time she reached the door, her two children had their luggage and were headed out on the porch. They carried all their stuff out to the front curb where they waited until a young man pulled to a stop in an old 1980 Chrysler New Yorker. They hurriedly loaded all their things into the trunk. She and the two kids quickly got into the car and the boy drove away from the front of the house.

Carl Otto

The young woman gave a long sigh of relief and said, "Johnnie, I hope this thing holds together until we get to our destination."

"Where you going, Mrs. Delaney?"

"Johnnie, I would just as soon keep that a secret. It's not that I don't trust you; it is just that I do not want to take any chances on Brad finding out where we are going."

"I understand, Mrs. Delaney, I think everybody around here knows about Mr. Delaney and nobody blames you for trying to get away from him, but what about the title to the car? I forgot to get it. How will I get it to you?"

"Don't worry about the title. I know your address. I will contact you later."

"I can drive by my house and get it now."

"I would much rather wait; I really need to get going. I will contact you in a few days."

Johnnie pulled the car over to the curb and stopped.

"Why are you stopping here, Johnnie?"

"I know you are in a hurry to get going; this is close to the highway and it's only about a mile from my home; I can walk from here."

"Oh, Johnnie, you are such a fine young man."

"Don't think anything of it, Mrs. Delaney; I like you guys a lot too."

Betty got out to go around to the driver's side. She

8

reached in her purse, pulled out an envelope and handed it to Johnnie.

"Oh, you don't need to pay for it until you get the title."

"Yes I do. Here you take the money. And as far as I am concerned, I would just as soon keep our little deal between the two of us."

"That's fine with me. I am just happy to help you. This car is old, but it runs good; just don't push it too hard. The tires are good and the brakes were overhauled just before I got it. And Tom, check the oil once in a while. It don't burn oil, but it has a leak around one of the gaskets."

"Okay Johnnie, I know how to check the oil."

"I know you do Tom. You know lots of stuff about cars."

Betty gave Johnnie a hug and got behind the wheel, as Tommie was getting in front seat with her. He looked in the back seat and said, "Cora, there is a seatbelt in the middle. Do you want up here too?"

"Yes, I want to be up with you guys." She scrambled over the seat.

Twenty minutes later, thirty-five year old Betty Delaney, her ten year-old son, Thomas, and her eight year-old Daughter, Cora, were pulling onto U.S. Highway 71 and were headed out of the metropolitan area. They were trying to escape an existence of brutality that was being inflicted on them by a husband and father who was becoming more and more dangerous as his drinking increased. Their problem had existed for some time; however, it had escalated lately, to the point Betty felt she and her children were in real danger.

It was taking Frank and Ben longer to finish putting the order together than they had anticipated, so Ben said, "Frank, I had better give Sue another call. I don't want her to be getting worried about me. She is a worry wart."

He called Sue to tell her it looked like he might not make it home until midnight or after. "You and the kids might as well go on to bed. I'll be there when we finish."

"I'll wait up for you."

"Now Sue, there is no need for you to wait up. You go on to bed. Just leave me a sandwich or something in the frig."

"You know better than that. I couldn't go to sleep anyway. I'll find something to do while I wait."

"Okay, I'll give you a ring on my cell phone when I leave the plant."

"You be careful. I love you."

"Love you too. See you later."

Ben went back to help Frank with the packing.

Betty was aware the old Chrysler was pretty well spent, but she never realized just how worn it might be until she glanced at the odometer; it read 192,562 miles.

My Peaceful Sunday

She thought, "Oh Lord, I hope this thing keeps running until we reach Little Rock. But, what could I expect for three hundred dollars."

The gasoline gage was not working, but Johnnie had promised the tank would be full when he brought it to her.

Suddenly it dawned on her, "I never thought to ask Johnnie if he had filled the tank, and I wonder if he put the extra oil in the trunk."

"What time is it Tommie?"

"That Bank sign we just passed said 9:35. Are we going drive all night, Mom?"

"We're not stopping for anything, unless we have to, until we put as many miles between ourselves and Kansas City as possible."

"Maybe you should drive a little faster, Mom. The speed limit is 70 and you're only going 50."

"Maybe I should speed up a bit; it seems to be running okay."

She increased the speed to sixty-five but at that speed they could feel something vibrating slightly and hear a strange noise.

Tommie said, "I think we better slow back down Mom. I don't like that strange sound."

"If you say so, Tommie. You know more about cars than I ever did know."

She reduced her speed to fifty-five.

Carl Otto

She was thinking, "Brad will surely figure I am headed for Wichita to be with my sisters. I realize he knows about my friend Brenda in Little Rock, but I cannot believe he would think I would go there."

"Mom, do you think maybe we should stop at the next gas station. It's possible that Johnnie forgot to fill the tank."

"You're right Tommie; we'll stop at the next station and convenience store, fill the tank and also get some snacks."

Betty was now headed south on highway 71. She drove another fifteen miles or so before she pulled off the highway and into a Conoco Quick Trip. She handed Tommie a ten dollar bill and told him to go get some bottled water and some snacks while she topped off the gas tank. She soon discovered Johnnie had indeed filled the tank; the nozzle kicked off after only three dollars and thirty cents. They all went to the restroom and then headed back south on highway 71.

Tommie checked the oil and discovered it was down only about a half quart.

He said, "The oil is okay Mom. And Johnnie put four quarts in the trunk."

"That's good Tommie."

She thought, "That Johnnie is a fine boy. He did everything he said he would do."

My Peaceful Sunday

Frank and Ben finished packing the last box just as the clock indicated 11:17 p.m. The driver for Franklin Tool had arrived earlier and was loading each box as the two men finished packing it.

"Ben, you go on home; the driver can help me load the rest of this stuff. And thanks for staying."

"No problem Frank. I'll see you Monday morning."

He gathered his stuff and headed for the parking lot; Frank and Ben's cars were the only remaining vehicles. He looked up into the night sky as he walked toward his vehicle.

Ben said aloud, "What a beautiful night."

And then he thought, "My, how lucky I am. I have a great wife and two super kids; I have a good job and a great boss; Sue is a nurse who works part time when she is needed. We own our home mortgage free. Life could not be better. I guess my cup does indeed runneth over."

He dialed his home number on the cell phone as he walked toward his car. The phone rang four times before Sue answered.

"Hi Ben. I'm sorry. I fell asleep in my recliner. How many times did the phone ring?"

"Oh Honey, don't say you're sorry for that. Anyway, I'm headed home. See you in a little bit."

"Okay, I'll warm up the soup."

Carl Otto

He got in his car and headed for the highway. He would travel about ten miles north of Carthage and then east two miles to his "line shack" as he jokingly calls it. It is an old farmhouse Sue and he remodeled ten years ago. They have the house and outbuildings on ten acres of what had once been a good sized farm. They all love the freedom of country living where the family they can raise a few calves, some chickens, and a goat. The family dog has free range and the barn is always home for at least three cats.

Ben was headed north on highway 71 when he noticed, in the lights of an approaching vehicle, a stopped car with the trunk lid up. He could see two children and a woman standing behind the stopped car. He slowed his own vehicle to get a better look. As he was a little past the stranded car he pulled off on the shoulder and stopped. He sat there for a moment. When another southbound car passed the stopped vehicle, he could plainly see the boy was trying to get something from the trunk.

My Peaceful Sunday

Ben looked north and south and could see no other vehicles approaching. So, he made a left turn, drove across the grass median and pulled to a stop behind the stranded car. Now he could plainly see a petite young woman and two young kids. And, they were looking at the left rear wheel. As he got out of his car he could see, from their facial expressions, they were all very frightened.

He said, "Mam, I just stopped because it looked like you could use some help. You have nothing to fear from me."

She answered, "There is something wrong with my car and I don't know what to do. Could you take a look at it?"

"Sure I can. Let me grab my flashlight."

When Ben got back to the car and observed the problem he could see it was a very serious one. He looked on the inside of the wheel where he observed the bearing was probably gone. The wheel was tipped in at the top and out at the bottom.

He said, "Mam, I hate to tell you this, but you are lucky you didn't lose that wheel while you were rolling."

The young woman just wilted down to a squatted position and started crying and the little girl went to her and also started crying. Ben was struck speechless.

Then the boy said, "My dad is a mean drunk and we are running away from home."

The woman was saying, "Oh my, what am I going to do? What will I do? I just bought this old car. I don't have the

Carl Otto

title or registration, I don't have it insured"

"Where are you from and where are you headed?"

Through uncontrollable sobs she answered, "We're — from — the — Kansas City metro area — and, we're headed for Little Rock."

"I hate to tell you this, but you won't be able to go another foot without getting this problem fixed."

She stood up and Ben was looking down on a petite woman who was at her wits end.

"But Sir, I – I – I –ah."

She could not hold her emotions as she broke down again.

Ben put his hand on her shoulder and said, "What is your name?"

The boy answered, "Her name is Betty Delaney and I'm her son Tom, and this is my little sister Cora."

"Betty, I don't know exactly what to do, but I will help you. It's approaching midnight so you and your kids can't be left out here all alone. First I need to call my wife and tell her I am going to be late."

Ben went back to his car and retrieved his cell phone from the front seat. He called Sue to tell her about the situation. They talked about what he might do.

After a few minutes, Sue said, "Ben, it is too late to do anything tonight, and you can't leave that young woman and those children out there by the highway."

My Peaceful Sunday

"What do you think I should do? She's afraid, because she has no title, registration or insurance on this old car."

"Bring them home with you. They can stay in the spare room tonight."

"Are you sure that's what you want me to do?"

"I can't see any other choice Ben."

"Okay Honey, I'll see what she thinks."

He walked back to the crippled car.

"Ms. Delaney. My wife has suggested you all come home with me and spend the night with us."

"Oh I can't impose on you like that. I will just wait until a trooper comes along and tell him the truth about the whole thing. Maybe there is a shelter house for battered families where he can take us."

"That might be what you will have to do, but not tonight. Now get your things. You are all coming home with me."

Ben opened his trunk and Tommie loaded all their stuff in his car. He glanced at his watch. It was 12:05 a.m. After the young woman had checked her car and locked the doors she looked up at Ben.

"Sir, It is hard for me to believe there is a man in this world willing to do what you are doing. You will never know how grateful I am. I don't even know your name"

"My name is Ben Wright, my wife is Susan and we have two children. Ben Jr., whom we call Butch, who is ten and

Carl Otto

our little girl, Jodie, is eight. We live in an old farmhouse about six miles from here."

She started sobbing again as she was trying to tell him how grateful she was. It was apparent the young woman was physically and emotionally exhausted. She was to the point where she was about to fall completely apart.

Ben took his right hand off the wheel and reached over to her shoulder.

"Betty. It is apparent to me that you have really been through the mill. Just close your eyes, take a deep breath and hold it for a moment."

Her son leaned forward and put his hand on her other shoulder, "It's gonna be okay Mom. Dad's not gonna beat us up any more. He don't know where we are and he probably don't care anyway."

Ten minutes later Ben was pulling to a stop in his back yard and Sue was coming out to meet them. She went to the passenger door as Betty started to get out.

"Hello, I am Ben's wife, Sue."

Betty started to say something as she stepped out of the car, then suddenly her speech began to slur and she started to fall. Susan grabbed her and her Cora started crying.

Sue called, "She has fainted, Ben!"

He hurried around the car and picked Betty up into his arms. As he started for the house he said, "Sue, should we take her to the hospital?"

My Peaceful Sunday

Sue answered, "No Ben, lets get her in the house and then get some liquids into her."

Being is a nurse, Sue knew what to do in these situations. She reassured Tommie and Cora that their mom had only fainted, "She is okay."

Ben carried her into the house and placed her tiny form on the couch with her feet up on the arm of the couch with her head lower. She began to regain consciousness immediately.

"Oh, my Lord, did I pass out?"

Sue said, "Yes, you fainted and was out for a few seconds. I would guess you are a bit dehydrated. And, it is only natural for this to happen when you are under a heavy strain. Don't worry. I am a nurse. You're fine now."

"I am so humiliated. I don't know what to say."

She sat up and started to say more.

Sue cut her off, "Now listen to me. You are just a young woman who needs a friend right now. And I am also a young woman who can always use a new friend. How about it?"

Sue held her arms out and Betty went to her. They embraced. It was hard for Sue to keep from crying too.

Ben said, "I don't know about the rest of you guys, but I am hungry."

Sue remarked, "I added a few cups of water to the soup after Ben and I decided to make a bed and breakfast out of

Carl Otto

this old farmhouse. Come on out in the kitchen; I think you are okay now."

She turned to Tommie and Cora, "Are you two hungry? I hope you like soup."

Tommie answered, "I like soup real good, and so does Cora."

Sue put four bowls on the table and began dishing up hot soup to their guests and Ben.

While Sue was filling the bowls, Tommie said, "Gosh I didn't know there was any people like you in the whole world. You don't know nothing about us and you still took us home with you, and now you're even feeding us."

Sue put her hand on his head and said, "Well Son, we claim to be Christians. I guess you and your mom and sister have come along to put us to the test. Don't you think that is how good Christians should treat one another?"

"I don't know very much about Christians, but if you people are Christians, then I think I want to be one too."

Sue leaned down and gave him a hug.

About that time, Jodie came into the kitchen dragging her pink blanket and rubbing her eyes. Butch was right behind her.

Half asleep, Butch said, "What's going on here. I didn't know we was gonna have company."

Ben said, "Butch and Jodie, this is Mrs. Delaney, Tommie and Cora. They are our new friends."

My Peaceful Sunday

Jodie stood silently for a moment before she said, "Cora, are you going to sleep with me?"

They all chuckled at that remark. Then Sue pulled Jodie to her side and said, "That will depend on what Mrs. Delaney says, but maybe we should just let all of them sleep in our guest room tonight."

Betty spoke up, "Yes I think I should just keep Tommie and Cora with me tonight. Is that okay with you Jodie?"

"Uh huh, it's okay."

Ben turned to Butch. "You take you little sister back upstairs and tuck her back in bed before she gets totally awake."

"Yeah I know Dad, If she gets plum wide awake, she'll keep the rest of us awake all night."

When they finished eating the soup, Sue showed Betty the guest room and the downstairs bathroom. Little Cora and Tommie were so sleepy they could hardly hold up their heads, so Betty put them to bed and then came back to the kitchen to visit with Sue and Ben.

 Ben stopped the visiting. "Betty, you have had a long hard trying day; I know you are exhausted. Let's all go to bed. Tomorrow is Sunday and we can sleep in. We'll talk at the breakfast table."

She started to cry again. Sue put her arms around Betty. "Betty, I am so glad it was Ben who came along and found you stranded out there on the highway. It will be okay."

Carl Otto

"Oh, you will never know how grateful I am. You people are so generous."

Ben interrupted again, "Come on now; let's hit the sack."

They said their good nights and went to bed.

Sue and Ben lay in the darkness for a minute or two before Ben felt her turn facing him. He gathered her into his arms and held her tight.

"You're and angel Sweetheart. I'm the luckiest man in the world."

"You're not so bad yourself, you Big Lug. I have never been prouder of you in my life than I am right now."

He squeezed her tighter. "Let's go to sleep."

Ben awoke at eight and turned toward Sue. She was gone. He could smell the coffee brewing as he dressed to go downstairs. When he entered the kitchen he saw Sue and Betty sitting at the table visiting.

Sue looked up and said, "Hi Sleepyhead. I was beginning to wonder if you were ever going to get up."

"My gosh, how long have you two been up?"

Betty spoke up, "I heard Sue rattling around in here about ten minutes ago so, I joined her."

"How are you feeling this morning Betty?"

"Oh I feel so much better. I really did sleep hard. I was so exhausted and frightened last night. I was almost ready for a straightjacket. But, then, out of the darkness, you suddenly appeared. It was like a guardian angel had been sent."

My Peaceful Sunday

"OH POOF! I'm anything but an angel. Here's the angel." He bent over and gave Sue a kiss.

"You're both angels."

Betty sat up straight as if she was startled by something. "Oh my, it has just occurred to me that I might be keeping you from going to church this morning."

Ben assured her, "Truthfully, I was going suggest we skip church this morning. I wanted to take my family for a drive in the country today, just to break the normal routine. But then you came along and took care of that problem. It's a lot more rewarding to be able to help someone who really needs a boost."

Sue spoke up. "Ben, do you think your dad could fix her car?"

"Of course he can. He's retired. But he is still a good mechanic. And, he still has that old wrecker he calls Huldie. I was thinking last night I would get Dad to tow Betty's car over to his place and I would help him fix it."

Betty looked down and shook her head. "This is unbelievable. You're even going to help me get my car fixed?"

"Yep, right after breakfast. I'm going to call my dad right now."

Ben called his dad and told him the basics of the problem.

His dad said, "Heck, I've been wondering what I would do today. I'll fire up old 'Huldie' and I'll be right over."

23

Carl Otto

They were all finishing breakfast when Ben's dad drove into the driveway with the old 1950 International, one ton pickup wrecker."

Ben said, "Betty, give me your keys and my dad and I will go get your car. We will take it over to his place. Sue can bring you and your kids over later."

"I still cannot believe there are people in this world like you folks."

"Betty, there are times in our lives when we have opportunities to be of service to others. This happens to be one of those times, and Sue and I are getting personal pleasure from this, as well as helping you, so don't you fret about it. Maybe someday you will be able to return the favor to someone else."

Ben went out and got in the old truck with his father.

As he got in, his dad said, "Well Son, I'm sure glad you found something for me to do today. Sounds like you have a real challenge for me."

"I don't think it is much of a challenge, but it will require some work."

"What do think is wrong with her car?"

"I don't think, I know what is wrong. The left rear wheel bearings are shot. I just hope the spindle isn't damaged too much."

"What model car is it?"

My Peaceful Sunday

"It is an older model; I think it is about a 1980 Chrysler New Yorker."

"One of them front wheel drive jobbers ain't it. I tell you what Son, if one side went out, you kin bet the other side ain't far behind it."

"I figured we would check the right side while we were at it."

As they pulled up to her stranded car, they could see a pickup was stopped in front of it. They got out to take a daylight look at the problem as a big burley fellow about six feet six and two hundred fifty pounds was getting out of the stopped pickup.

He started toward them saying, "Do you guys happen to know where the woman and two kids are who were in this car."

Before Ben could answer, his dad said, "They're with my son's wife at his place. Seems they had a little breakdown and Ben came to their rescue."

He extended his hand and said, "I'm Ellery Wright, Ben's dad. Who are you?"

Ben was thinking, "Oh crimeny crunch, I didn't tell Dad the whole story. This guy has got to be Betty's husband."

The man ignored Ellery's hand and came toward Ben, "Where have you got my woman and kids?"

Carl Otto

"Hey Buddy, I don't have 'your' woman and kids! I did offer to help a young woman and two kids —"

He cut Ben off, as he got right in his face.

Ben was backing up as the big man snarled, "Listen Fella. That little snipe took my two brats and flew the coop, and I have come to take her back home."

Ben kept trying to avoid a confrontation.

Backing away, he said, "You can't be talking about the woman and kids I helped last night."

While Ben was trying to talk to this "lump of ignorance," with booze on his breath, his dad went back to his truck, reached under the seat and retrieved his old Peace Maker six-shooter. Ben saw him slip up behind the guy and level his pistol at him.

"Ok Loudmouth, just back off before I fill your drunken carcus full of holes."

The man turned toward Ellery and snarled, "You wrinkled old prune. I think I'll just take that pea shooter away from you and jam it down your throat."

"I wouldn't advise that move Fella. I know how to use this thing, and I don't miss."

The guy made a move toward Ellery as he lowered the barrel and fired a round into the pavement between the big man's feet.

"You better cool it, Big Fella; the next one will make a hole in your leg."

My Peaceful Sunday

This huge man did hesitate a second or two. He then made a lunge toward Ellery.

Ben's dad was not fooling around. He fired a shot into the man's right thigh and the guy went down like a dropped sack of sand. He was moaning with pain and cursing Ellery, as the blood began to spurt out of his lag. He tried to get to his feet, but fell to the pavement.

Ellery, while still holding his pistol, said, "You better cool it, Meathead, 'cause the next one will be right between your eyes."

All the while this scene was taking place, another car had stopped behind the wrecker and two men had gotten out. They were witnesses to the entire scene. One of them went to the wounded man's side saying,

Carl Otto

"You had better settle down Man and let us get the bleeding stopped."

The wounded drunk took a swing at the man who was trying to help, so the guy just stepped back and said, "Okay Buddy, just go ahead and bleed to death. It's no skin off my nose. Looks to me like you have gotten about what you deserve."

The stranger then turned to Ellery and said, "I saw the whole thing. If this drunk dies, I'll swear it was self defense."

And the other man with him repeated the same thing.

The wounded drunk tried to get up again but his leg crumpled under his weight. It was obvious the shot had really weakened his leg; possibly shattered his femur.

Ben went to him again pleading, "Let us help you. You are bleeding badly. This is serious."

He spat in Ben's face.

Ben stepped back saying, "No wonder your wife wanted to get herself and those kids away from you. You are nothing but a savage animal."

Ben turned to the two men who had stopped. "I guess we will just wait until he loses enough blood to pass out. I called 911 while you guys were trying to reason with him."

One of the onlookers said, "Don't anyone strike a match; there is so much alcohol fumes coming from this nut, it could cause an explosion."

While all this was taking place, a State Trooper had ap-

28

My Peaceful Sunday

proached the scene from the south. He drove his patrol car across the median and stopped on the shoulder of the road. Ben went directly to the trooper and told him they were trying to help the guy, but he refused.

The trooper asked, "What happened?"

Ellery spoke up. "This big loudmouth was threatening my son, so I got my gun and tried to stop him. Then he turned on me. I fired one warning shot, but the stupid fool kept coming, so I shot him in the leg."

One of the two witnesses told the trooper, "It was self defense. We saw the whole thing. He wouldn't listen to reason. The old man was simply defending himself. We have all been trying to help him, but all he does is curse and spit at us."

Ben's mind was in a whirl. All he could think about was, "What in the world is going to happen to Dad now. He is eighty-two years old and has never been in any kind of trouble. Now he has shot somebody, and the guy could die."

Ellery was still standing with his old six shooter hanging in his hand by his side when the trooper said, "Let me have your weapon Sir."

"Oh no, I have had this old Peace Maker for fifty years and I ain't givin it up to anybody. I'll put it back under my truck seat where I always keep it."

Ben went to his dad and said, "Dad, this is a different situation now. You will have to give up your gun."

Carl Otto

"It wasn't my fault that this crazy fool tried to attack me. All I was doin is defending you and myself."

The trooper told Ellery, "Sir, from what these witnesses say, you were doing just that; however, anytime someone gets shot like this there has to be an investigation."

While all this was going on, the big drunk was beginning to get weaker and show signs of passing out. The pool of blood in which he lay looked like he could not have much left. The trooper turned his attention to keeping the traffic moving. Several cars had already stopped.

It was a good twenty minutes before the ambulance arrived. The big guy had passed out. The ambulance crew immediately started an IV on him before they even tried to load him onto the stretcher. When they did finally get him loaded into the ambulance, it looked as if he were a goner.

The ambulance was leaving the scene as a fire truck pulled up and began washing the blood off the highway. Ben had talked his dad into relinquishing his handgun to the local sheriff who had also arrived a few minutes earlier.

Ellery and the sheriff were personal friends, so Ben was happy to see him show up; however, he was not very pleased to see a TV camera crew arrive and start taking pictures and asking for interviews.

Ben thought, "Oh good Lord. I was looking forward to a peaceful Sunday with my family."

The sheriff was talking to Ellery when he motioned for

My Peaceful Sunday

Ben to come to them. The sheriff had told the TV crew he would talk to them in a minute.

He turned to Ben and said, "Ben, I have been discussing this situation with Ellery. This is what I have decided: I am going take statements from the two witnesses so they can to go on their way for now. You and your dad may go ahead with your plans to fix this lady's car. Then Monday morning I want both of you to show up at my office at eight o'clock. How does that sound?"

"That sounds more than fair to me; how about you Dad?"

"Son, don't you have to be at work Monday morning?"

"I'll call Fred; he'll understand."

"Then it suits me fine. We will be in your office early Monday morning."

The sheriff added, "Don't be too concerned about that guy. He has lost a lot of blood, but he will survive."

Ellery responded, "I don't give a hoot if he does die. The world would be a lot better off if we didn't have people like him around."

"You are probably right Ellery, but you better hope he does live; there will be a lot fewer headaches over it. Now hand me your gun; I'll get it back to you when this is all cleared up."

The sheriff then turned his attention to the TV crew and Ben and Ellery turned their attention to getting Betty's car

Carl Otto

towed to his dad's place. Ellery turned his wrecker around and backed up to the rear of the car and Ben hooked up the lift apparatus. He then made sure the car was in neutral before he got in the truck cab with his dad.

They started towing the car away. Ben looked at his watch; it was 11:17 a.m.

He said, "Let's just go to my house first, Dad. We can grab a bite to eat before we get started on this project. And besides, I have to tell that young woman what has happened."

"Oh good Lord Son, I don't envy you having to do that chore."

They approached Ben's place just in time; Sue, Betty and the four kids were just getting ready to board the family car and drive over to Ellery's place. They had fixed a picnic lunch for everybody.

Sue looked up as they pulled in the circle drive.

"I see you already have her car fixed."

"No, we haven't started yet; we got sidetracked a little."

"Oh you did. What happened?"

Ben didn't know exactly how to approach telling Betty, but he knew he had to do it somehow. So he just went to her and said, "Betty, your husband was already there, waiting in his pickup when we pulled up behind your car."

A look of sheer terror came to her face as she put her hands to her mouth. "Oh my goodness! He has already found us. Where is he now?"

32

My Peaceful Sunday

Before Ben could answer, his dad said, "He's in the hospital because I put a bullet in his leg."

Sue said, "Dad! You shot him?"

"Yes, I shot him. He tried to attack both of us. I warned him but he wouldn't stop, so I shot him."

Tommie blurted, "Good! I hope he is dead."

Betty asked, "How bad is he?"

"Dad shot him in the leg, and he lost a lot of blood, but the Sheriff doesn't think the wound will be fatal."

Sue suggested they all go back into the house, so they did.

Ben told Betty, "Dad and I are still going to repair your car. We might not get it finished in time for you to go on your way today, but you can leave here in the morning if you wish."

"Do you think I should go talk to the sheriff?"

"I don't know about that. I do think you should have a legal restraining order served on your husband."

"I wonder how he found where we went so quickly."

"That makes no difference. The fact is, he is now in the hospital, and he will surely be there for several days, if not longer."

While they were discussing what course of action might be best for Betty and the kids, the Sheriff pulled into the driveway. Ben got up and went outside to meet him.

"Ben there has been another development in this case."

"What now Sheriff?"

Carl Otto

"The ambulance crew got that guy to the hospital okay. They took him to the emergency room and started the tests so they could give him a blood transfusion. I guess the IV fluids must have revived him a little, because while they were trying to work on him he woke up and went nuts again. He pulled all the tubes out and started cussing and spitting at everybody. Then suddenly he grabbed his chest and fell to the floor. He died of a massive heart attack."

"Holy cow! He died! Now what is going to happen to Dad?"

"Nothing is going to happen to your dad."

"Are you serious, Sheriff?"

The sheriff answered, "I was there, and I discussed the entire scenario with the doctors. They said his death had nothing to do with the leg injury, and I suggested they not even mention the gun-shot wound on his death certificate."

"Sheriff, you are serious!"

"I am serious. Sometimes even the law can be bent a little; we call it discretional latitude. As far as I am concerned, this case is closed."

Ben went back in the house and they all stood in silence, awaiting his report.

"Betty, your husband died of a massive heart attack in the hospital emergency room. The doctors told the sheriff it had nothing to do with his being shot, so the gunshot

My Peaceful Sunday

wound will not be mentioned on his death certificate. The sheriff said the case is closed."

"Really! Are you sure that's what he meant?"

"As sure as I have ever been about anything."

"In other words, I am free to go back to my home if that is what I chose."

"You are not going to have to worry about being abused any more."

Sue spoke up. "Betty, do you have family or friends where you live who can help you get everything straightened out"

"As a matter of fact, I have Brad's sister and her husband, Don, who will help. One time Don tried to talk to Brad about the way he was treating the kids and me, and Brad beat him up and told him to keep his nose out of his business."

Sue answered, "It's even better if his people understand."

"Oh they all knew him quite well. None of them could understand why he was so mean. He is the only one in their entire family like that."

Sue turned to Ben. "Ben, do you mean the sheriff is overlooking the fact that dad had a gun and actually shot somebody?"

"I think his term for overlooking the shooting incident was, 'discretional latitude,' whatever that means. He did take dad's pistol and he never mentioned to me whether he would get it back or not."

Ellery spoke up, "Yes he did Son, he told me I could have

Carl Otto

it back as soon as all this is cleared up. So, I guess I'll get it back the next time I see him."

Sue remarked, "I guess they are not quite good ole boy, old west lawmen, but it looks like the sheriff has decided to handle the matter in that way."

Ben suggested, "Okay, lets eat those sandwiches so Dad and I can go ahead and start on the car.

Betty asked, "Would it be alright if I go back in the bedroom for a little while with my kids. I think we need to have a talk."

"Why of course it is Betty. Ben and I and Grandpa will go ahead and grab a bite. You take as long as you want. You and the kids can eat later."

After she and her kids had gone into the house, Sue turned to Ben, saying, "Oh my Ben, what a terrible experience that young woman has been through. It's obvious she wanted free from that man, but I am sure she did not want it to happen like it did."

Ellery spoke up, "I'm not sure about that, Sue. The man was never going to change. That little woman thought she had gotten away from him, but it didn't take him twenty-four hours to find her. To be perfectly honest, I felt worse about shooting Japs, during the war than I do about shooting that dummy. And I don't think I would be sorry if I had shot the stupid fool right between the eyes."

"Well Dad, at least it wasn't the gunshot that killed him."

My Peaceful Sunday

"Like I said, it makes no difference to me. I would feel worse about shooting a coyote."

Ben added, "Dad, I have a feeling that Betty might be upset over the whole thing; however, as bad as it is, I would almost bet she is secretly happy it is finally over."

Sue turned toward the house, "I can only imagine what she is thinking, but I think you're right. I too would bet she is happy she is free. But, let's drop this conversation. It is beginning to make me sick."

An hour later Ellery and Ben had Betty's car at Ellery's place and had removed the damaged wheel. They discovered the spindle was not damaged so they removed the wheel from the other side and found those bearings were also getting bad.

"Let's go to a parts store and pick up what we need Ben. I'll pay for the stuff. That little woman doesn't need to know anything about what they cost. As far as she is concerned we simply fixed what was already there and didn't have to buy anything."

"That sounds like a good plan, Dad."

It was 5:30 p.m. by the time Ben was headed back to his house with Betty's car. It took them a little longer than they had anticipated, but his dad insisted they also service the car completely. The first thing he did was fire up his steam cleaner and remove all the grease and dirt off the engine and all around it.

Carl Otto

Then they not only replaced the back wheel bearings, but also changed the oil, changed the oil, air and transmission filters, greased all the fittings, checked all fluid levels, tightened all the cover plates so the oil leaks were stopped, put on a new serpentine belt and a new set of spark plugs and filled the gas tank. He even fixed a loose connection on the gas gage, so it was now working.

Ben was thinking as he drove along, "I'm glad the tires and the brakes were good; he probably also would have insisted on a new set of tires and a brake job."

Betty, Sue and the four kids came out to meet Ben when he drove Betty's car into the back yard driveway.

The first thing Betty said was, "Now I want to know how much those repairs cost. I want to pay you for whatever you have been out."

"Betty, you don't need to worry about that, I have not been out one cent. Dad is a retired mechanic, and you would be amazed at how much stuff he has for fixing cars; especially older models."

Ben might have had Betty fooled about how much work they had done on the car, but he didn't fool Tommie. Tommie was only ten years old but he was wise little guy.

As soon as he could get Ben aside, he said, "Mom don't know nothing about cars, but I do. I raised the hood and took a look. You guys made that old engine look like a new one. You said it didn't cost you one cent, but I could tell it

My Peaceful Sunday

was runnin a lot better than before. That belt wasn't squeekin anymore and the gas gauge works, and your dad must have tuned it up and stopped those oil leaks. And besides, you might have said it didn't cost you nothing but you didn't mention how much it cost your dad."

Ben leaned down to Tommie. "You are indeed a sharp little guy. And yes, I didn't mention what it cost my dad. As a matter of fact he didn't even tell me what it cost him, but he has the money to do those things, and he really enjoyed doing it. Why, he even had a chance to fire up his old steam cleaner he hadn't used for years. He loves to work on cars. So we don't want to take an old man's pleasures away from him, do we?"

"I guess not. He must be a good old dude."

"He is a good old dude."

Betty decided to go back to where she lived in the Kansas City area, but she is not going to stay there. She and Sue have talked about employment opportunities in the Carthage and Joplin area so she has decided she will come back down to this area as soon as she has all her business finished.

She and the kids stayed one more night. Ben was getting ready to leave for work the following morning, when Betty came out of the bedroom. She came over to him to tell him again how grateful she was.

He stopped her. "Betty, as I have said before, I hope some day you'll have a chance to help a total stranger who is having a problem, because you cannot imagine how much pleasure I have gotten, and my dad has gotten, out of the past thirty-six hours. You don't owe us a thing; we owe you."

He reached out and pulled her to him and gave her a long hug. Then he hugged and kissed Sue as he left the house. Ben wasn't kidding when he told Betty he had gotten pleasure from what he had done. He knew his chest was a little higher and his feet were a little lighter as he went to his car.

He thought, "Wow! I really did have peaceful Sunday after all. I guess the Lord had other plans for me. I am saddened a man had to lose his life because he refused to change a lifestyle that was slowly killing him anyway, and I'm sorry dad had to take the action he took, but I do not regret what he did. That man's brain was pickled beyond repair.

Wow! What an experience. In my wildest dreams, I never would have thought I'd be faced with something like the past week-end. I wonder what Frank will think when I tell him about what happened. I'll bet Reverend Flanegan might even consider our helping Betty and her kids a good excuse for missing church."

THE END

WET PANTS

O rville and Ethel Flynn are getting ready to drive to the Community Center where their nine children are hosting a Golden Wedding Anniversary Party in celebration of the fifty years their parents have been married. Ethel is really excited about the affair, and, so is Orville; however, he is acting like he is bored to death.

Orville is complaining, "Oh, Ethel, why do I have to put this dad blamed tie on. I'll bet ninety percent of all the guys who come there today won't be wearing a tie."

"Now listen to me, you Old Geezer, you will be the only guy there who is celebrating his golden wedding anniversary, and I want you to look nice."

Carl Otto

"You sure have turned into a bossy old woman."

"Huh, just wait 'til we have our diamond anniversary."

"Diamond? When will that be?"

"When we are married seventy-five years."

He put both hands to the sides of his head and said, "Oh Lord. I'm not sure I can put up with you for another twenty-five years."

She made the final tug on his tie and straightened the knot. "Don't you remember when the preacher said, 'until death do you part,' and you said, 'I do?'"

He put his arms around her and hugged her close as he said, "You dad blamed right I remember. And, I have never quit loving you since we were in the sixth grade together. There have been some times when I sure didn't like you, but I have always loved you."

"The sixth grade? I have loved you ever since we were in the fifth grade together."

He kissed her and continued, "Isn't it a shame we didn't get married while we were in grade school; we could be having our sixtieth anniversary instead of this dinky fiftieth."

"Yes, and we could have a dozen or more kids sponsoring it instead of just nine."

He answered, "I think we got married soon enough. Let's go get in the car; they are probably waiting on us."

When they arrived, their kids were lined up in the order in which they were born with 34 yr. old Orville Jr. first, fol-

Wet Pants

lowed by, 32 yr old Emily, 30 yr. old Oscar, 28 yr. old Edith, the 25 yr old twins, Owen and Elsie , 23 yr old Elizabeth, 21 yr. old Esther, 19 yr old Elvis.

A wife of one of the guests remarked to her husband, "Oh my goodness, just look at how all those offspring are greeting their parents. They sure are a nice Catholic family."

"They aren't Catholics."

"They aren't?"

"No. I once heard a fellow ask Orville if they were Catholics and he answered, in his slow drawl, 'Nah, we're just careless Protestants.' But, with regard to your remark, they really are a nice family. There is quite a story about how that love affair first started."

He wife answered, "Oh, is that right? Tell me about it."

No, I don't want to spoil it when Emily tells it to the whole group later on, after dinner."

And, so the celebration continued as everyone went through the cafeteria to pick up their plates and seat themselves at a table. The building was buzzing with friendly conversation and laughter when Emily stood and pecked her fork on her water glass several times in order to get everyone's attention.

When all had quieted down, Emily made the official welcome.

She started by saying, "I was drafted to be the master of ceremonies because Buddy, referring to her older brother,

Carl Otto

Orville Jr., told all the rest of the family I was better quali-
fied for the job because I once made an A on a high school
Speech Class assignment."

She continued, "The assignment was to prepare and
make a presentation speech."

Pause. "I presented a classmate with a mousetrap, because she had been telling me about how she would wake up
in the middle of the night with a mouse in bed with her."

"However, that has nothing to do with today's event. The
first thing I am going to do is tell all of you why our dad fell
in love with our mom. They were both in the sixth grade
- — -.'"

At that point, her father interrupted, as he stood at his
chair and said, "Hold everything, Em. I know what you're
going to tell. So, you sit down, because I am going to tell it
myself."

He walked to the middle of the table and replaced Emily
at the podium.

There was a long pause in which the crowd quieted until
you could hear a pin drop.

He continued, "Several years ago, at a family get-togeth-
er, I think I made the mistake of telling this batch of youngins of ours, a story; a true story. And, I guess, now that I'm
an old man who is not too concerned about being embarrassed, I will tell all of you about it."

Wet Pants

He cleared his throat and continued, "You see, Ethel and I have been together ever since we were in the first grade. I didn't realize it at the time, but Ethel fell in love with me before the first week of that first year ended."

Ethel called out loudly, "I did not. I was in the fifth grade before I fell in love with him."

He turned toward his wife, "Thanks Ethel. I stand corrected – again."

Continuing, he said, "We were in the sixth grade, and I was nearly thirteen years old. I don't remember exactly what we were doing, but we were working on an assignment when I began to feel the need to go to the bathroom. I raised my hand with my index finger showing, indicating I had to go. Back then it was, One finger for number one and two fingers for number two; maybe it still is; I don't know.

The teacher told me it hadn't been twenty minutes since recess, so I could wait until later.

I really thought I could — -- right up the point when my bladder sphincter relaxed, just a tad. Now, here I am, almost thirteen years old; I haven't peed my pants since I was three.

Once that sphincter started to relax, I lost all control of it. It flat opened the floodgate and I could feel that warm liquid wet the front of my pants and run down all around my bottom on the seat.

Carl Otto

Then it started running off the back of my seat and splattering on the floor. I stretched my foot back so the pee could hit the back of my heel and run down my shoe instead of making a noise as it hit the floor."

By now he had to stop telling the story ever little bit to allow the laughter to subside before he could continue.

"So, there I sat, a twelve year old boy with wet pants and a puddle on the floor beneath my seat. Can you imagine anything more embarrassing? I tell you I wanted to die. All I could think about was, 'Oh Lord, please help me.' What in the world was I going to do?

Nobody noticed the puddle on the floor or the pained look in my face, except Ethel. When she saw what had happened, she raised her hand and told the teacher she was finished with her assignment and asked if she could work on her water coloring. The teacher gave her permission to do so.

So Ethel rose to her feet, went to the sink and drew a quart jar of water. As she returned to her seat, she came by where I was sitting and hoping I would die.

Suddenly Ethel tripped and started to fall; as she did so she dumped the entire big jar of water in my lap.

She immediately began to say how sorry she was, as all the other kids began to laugh, and even make fun of her for being so clumsy.

The teacher told me to go on down to the gym and put on my gym shorts or some sweat pants. I didn't wait for a

Wet Pants

second invitation; I high tailed it out of there.

The custodian was called to mop up the mess and class went on.

At lunchtime I quietly walked over to Ethel and said, "You did that on purpose, didn't you?"

She whispered, "I peed my pants once last year, and I was in a store, shopping with my mom. I wanted to die; I don't know what I would have done if it had been at school."

Orville continued, "Now let me ask you folks. How could anyone not fall madly in love with someone who would do that for them? Before the day I peed my pants, I really liked Ethel, but I have been in love with her ever since that day."

Ethel stood and hugged Orville when he came back to the seat.

Emily stepped to the microphone. When all was quiet again she said, "Thanks Dad, for telling that story. Actually, I had a totally different story in mind; that's the first time I have ever heard that one. Do any of the rest of you guys remember dad telling that before?"

All her siblings emphatically shook their heads, 'no.'

THE END

Note: I got the idea for the above story from an email sent to me by Judy Flanegan, a Methodist Minister in Iowa who is one of my former students.

GRANDPA BERN'S HOTEL

GRANDPA BERN'S HOTEL

Woodrow "Woodie" Bern's grandpa is an independent old cuss who insists on living by himself in an old rundown cabin near the Elk River. He loves to fish and he is content to be without the so-called, "necessities" of modern day living. It is not that he has to live this way, because he owns a nice home within two miles of the cabin. And, he goes back to his home once or twice a week to shower, wash his clothes and check things out. But then he returns to the cabin as soon as he can. He does have a cell phone; however, generally does not keep it with him and he forgets to plug in into the charger, so the battery is dead much of the time.

Four years ago, when Woodie's grandfather reached the age of eighty, Woodie asked him, "Grandpa. How does it feel to be an Octogenarian?"

The old fellow replied, "I ain't what ever that fancy word you used is, I am a Ozark American. That is politically correct for, Hillbilly, and I'm proud of it."

Grandpa Bern living in that cabin is usually not much of a problem because his family members know he is healthy and he is very innovative. So as long as he is happy, none of them try to change him. However, the latest crazy weather patterns have given some of them a reason to worry about him. They are all aware what could happen during extreme

Carl Otto

weather times, because during the summer of 1951, that cabin was completely surrounded by water with only the roof and the fireplace chimney sticking out above the flood, and Woodie is afraid it could happen again.

With global warming and all its ramifications, it is difficult for even the most astute meteorologist to make weather predictions in which one can place much trust. The most recent weather report indicates heavy rains in south central and southeast Kansas that could turn to freezing rain or even snow. If it does snow, the amounts could be record breaking. In view of what he had been hearing, Woodie tried to contact his grandfather; however, every time he tried to reach his grandpa on the cell phone all he got was a message saying the phone was not turned on. So he decided to drive down there and spend the weekend with his grandfather. He figured he would first go by the house, just in case his grandpa happened be there.

It was raining when Woodie left his home in Wichita. He had invited his wife and two kids to accompany him on the trip, but she and her sister had made other plans; she and the kids declined the offer, so Woddie struck out on his own. By the time he reached Howard, the rain had started to fall so heavily his wipers could not handle it; he had to slow down his speed considerably in order to see the road, and at one time, actually pulled over on the shoulder and

54

Grandpa Bern's Hotel

stopped for a while. He seemed to be driving along as if he were under a waterfall.

He was thinking, "Oh I hope that old geezer has gone to the house. This rain is going to have that cabin under water again."

Woodie turned his radio to a Coffeyville station as the announcer was saying, "This looks like it could be one of the heaviest rain falls we have seen in this area in years. Already there are numerous reports of water over the roads. There are closings and cancellations faster than we can announce their locations. If you do not need to be out in this storm, please stay home."

The announcement was followed with a list of closings. The time was 4:30 pm. Among the closings was the cancellation of a Junior Senior Prom that was to be held that very evening.

Woodie thought, "It might be a little late for that bit of information. I don't envy the sponsors of that event. They could be stuck with a gym full of kids to supervise until the water recedes."

By the time he reached the gravel road that leads to his grandfather's house, the ditches were running bank full and the water was across the road in several places. He looked at the outside temperature gauge on his rear view mirror; the temp was 40 degrees. So, at least it looked like the predictions of a possible snow might be wrong

Carl Otto

The rainfall was so heavy and the wind was blowing it around to the extent that even the most experienced driver would have had difficulty. Soon Woodie could see the yard light at his grandfather's house and there were lights in the kitchen windows.

He said aloud, "Oh great! He has decided to come to the house."

As he pulled into the parking area between the house and the barn, he could see a vehicle parked near the yard fence gate. He pulled alongside the other vehicle and got out of his car. At that point he realized the vehicle was not his grandfather's.

The engine of the car was running and there appeared to be people in the car. Woodie hurried through the downpour to the kitchen door and entered.

Opening the door, he was surprised to see a big strong looking boy, dressed in a suit. The boy was as shocked to see Woody as he was to see the boy.

He said, "Oh Mister, I'm sorry I just came on in, but I knocked and nobody answered and the door was unlocked, and we are lost. We didn't intend to take anything."

"Are you the only one here?"

"Yes, I think so. There are three more of us out in my car. We were headed to our high school when we heard on the radio the prom was cancelled. We shouldn't have done it, but we decided to drive around for a while. Then

Grandpa Bern's Hotel

the rain started coming real fast and we got lost. We saw the yard light, so we came here. I knocked several times, but nobody answered, so I guessed there was nobody home. Is this your house?"

"No, this place belongs to my grandfather, but you say nobody else is here?"

"I really don't know. Nobody has answered my calls. I found the light switch and turned it on. We didn't intend to do anything to stuff."

"That's okay Son. I believe you. But I am concerned about my grandfather. Have you looked around the house?"

"No, I have been in this room only."

Woodie took a quick look around the house, but his grandpa was nowhere to be seen.

Woodie said, "I noticed there are others in your car. How many?"

"There are four of us."

"You better go tell the rest of them to come on in. The way this rain is falling right now, you are not going anywhere. The water is already running ditch full and over the road in several places"

"Do you really think so?"

"Son, this is a full-blown Kansas flood right now. Even If it lets up in an hour or so, you won't be able to go anywhere until the water runs off. We are fortunate this house sits on high ground, because in flood times it would otherwise be

Carl Otto

under water. The water is already over the road out of here, and it is rising. Go tell your friends to come in the house."

He thought, "I'll try his cell phone one more time."

This time his grandfather answered.

"Grandpa! Oh am I glad to hear your voice. Are you still down there in the cabin?"

"No. I'm headed back to the house. Where are you?"

"I'm in your kitchen"

"Great! I'm glad you came for a visit. Are you alone?"

"Not exactly. Where are you right now, Grandpa?"

"I'm pulling into my back yard."

The other three kids had all hurried to the house and were standing in the kitchen when Woodie's grandfather entered the room.

He got a puzzled look, as he saw all the youngsters. "What the dickens are you doing out here with all these kids?"

Woodie explained why the kids were there and why he had come down to check things out.

His Grandfather's reply was, "I'm glad to see you, but I don't need no checking up on. I can take care of myself."

One of the girls asked Woodie, "Mr. could I use your cell phone to call my parents?"

"Of course. You may all use it. Or you may use Grandpa's telephone that is located just around the corner, in the next room. You all need to call your parents."

Grandpa Bern's Hotel

Grandpa looked at the girls and shook his head. "Good Lord! Don't you girls know better than to be out on a day like this dressed in outfits like that?"

"We were going to the prom." One of them answered.

"Do you girls call them wrap around drapes on your shoulders, jackets? My Lord you're practically naked from the waist up."

Woodie spoke up. "Now Grandpa, these girls are dressed properly for the occasion. It is just that the occasion was cancelled."

"They ain't no occasion, that's proper, for young girls to run around, half- naked. Do your mommas know you're outside dressed like that?"

Woodie looked at one of the girls and noticed her lower lip was quivering and she was about to break down and cry.

"Don't let him worry you Honey, his bark is a lot worse than his bite."

She answered, "That's exactly what my grandpa said about this formal."

Grandpa spoke up. "I'll tell you one thing, this rain storm is a real doozie. I don't know where you kids live, but you're not getting home tonight. Now tell me what your names are."

One of the boys spoke up. "My name is James Bishop; this is Sara Jinkins; this is Bob Reynolds and this is Kendra Myers."

Carl Otto

Grandpa answered, "Well, my name is Woodrow Bern, but you kin all call me Grandpa and this is my grandson Woodie Bern. Actually he was named after me, but we call him Woodie. Have you kids had anything to eat?"

Bob answered, "We were supposed to have a meal at the prom, but since it got called off, we ain't had anything."

"Well, I tell you what. I have a big mess of chili in one of them plastic containers in the icebox. I think if I warm it up and add a couple more cans of beans, there will be enough for all of us. Now make your phone calls and tell your folks you are safe and sound at Grandpa Bern's hotel?"

Then he continued, "Oh yes. All you kids need to get into some dry clothes. You girls look like you're about the same size as Grandma was, so you go in that bedroom." He pointed to a door and continued, "Where you'll find a whole closet full of clothes. Just pick out what ever suits you. And the top drawer of that chest has some flannel sleeping gowns for later on. And you boys kin put on some of my stuff, right there in that hall closet. And, by the way, I don't like being called Mister; so all you kids just call me Grandpa."

Woodie called home to let his wife know the situation and the kids all contacted their parents. All but Bob's parents wanted to talk to Woodie to verify where their kids were. Kendra's mother seemed to be the most apprehensive about the situation until she was assured that

Grandpa Bern's Hotel

Mr. Bern had plenty of room for everybody. The girls would have to share a room and the boys would share another. Both men were honorable individuals who would properly supervise the kids.

The girls were in the bedroom for a good thirty minutes before Grandpa yelled at them, "Come on girls, the chili is ready; you ought to have found something by now."

The door opened and the girls stepped out. Sara had selected a pink sweat pant and sweater outfit and Kendra was wearing a light green sweat pant and sweater outfit. As they walked into the room Grandpa turned toward them. He dropped the stirring spoon he was holding.

"Oh my." His voice began to falter. "You girls have picked Fern's two favorite outfits. Oh my, you look good in them." His voice broke as he bent over to pick up the spoon he had dropped.

Woodie said, "Grandma passed away nearly five years ago, but he still misses her."

"Yeah Woodie, a day never passes that I don't think about her. And seeing those girls just now, kinda shook out a few old memories."

Kendra asked, "Would you rather we put on something else?"

"Oh no, girls. I'm glad you picked them outfits. As a matter of fact, you look so nice in them that I want you to keep them."

Carl Otto

Both girls said, "Oh, we couldn't do that."

Grandpa insisted, "Yes you can. You could see that closet was full of clothes. I've been wondering what to do with them anyway."

The boys had both dawned a flannel shirt and a pair of bib overalls.

"And you boys keep them overalls and flannel shirts; I have growed out of them anyway. And, since you two dudes look like hired hands now, I guess it's time I put you to work. Go in yonder in the dining room and fetch two more chairs. I think we can all crowd around the kitchen table."

He placed the big pot of chili in the middle of the table and got a box of soda crackers from the pantry and directed the girls to get some bowls and spoons from the cupboard.

"One of you grab that half gallon of orange juice and that big bottle of catsup from the ice box."

Sara looked around the kitchen and then asked, "Where is the ice box?"

Woodie leaned close to her and said, "The ice box is a grandpa term for the refrigerator."

With everything on the table, Grandpa sat down at one end of the table and Woddie sat at the other end. Jim and Sara sat on one side and Kendra and Bob sat on the other side.

Grandpa reached both hands out and said, "Let's all join hands while I ask the blessing."

Grandpa Bern's Hotel

It was apparent all the kids were from families who asked blessings before meals because they seemed to know what to do.

Kendra asked, "May I ask the blessing?"

"Course ya kin youngin."

"Dear Heavenly Father, we thank you for good people, because I don't know what would have happened to us if we hadn't come to this old farm house, where this man, Mr. Woddie and his grandpa are helping us. Lord, Bob didn't mean to come in uninvited, but it was cold and raining hard and we were about to get stuck, and the door was unlocked. And now Sara and I have warm clothes on instead of those fancy formal dresses. And this old man, Grandpa, has fixed all of us a good dinner. Bless the chili and Grandpa who fixed it. Amen."

As they released grips on one another, Woodie said, "Kendra, that was a nice blessing."

Sara stood and started dipping the chili into their individual bowls, as grandpa got up and headed for the pantry.

"Oh, I forgot the vinegar and sugar. Grandma always said that a bowl of chili or a bowl of soup needed a teaspoon of sugar to give it that special flavor. I didn't put any in the mix cause I thought some of you might not like it."

Jim remarked, "I never heard of putting sugar in chili before. I do usually add a little vinegar."

Carl Otto

"Oh kids, you ain't never tasted good chili until you get a bite of mine with a teaspoon full of sugar stirred into it."

Kendra said, "I think I'll try it."

"And there ain't no salt in it either. I figger ya can always add a little salt, but ya shore cain't take it out, onc't it's in there. And I like to add a pinch of Garlic salt."

While the six of them ate and visited, Woodie could not help but think, "If all the young people in the world were half as nice as these four kids, we would have no worries about the future."

They talked about goals in life. Every one of the youngsters intended to go to the local Community College for two years while they made final plans before going on to four-year institutions. And, as they ate and visited, Grandpa discovered he was acquainted with at least one close relative of every one of the kids.

When they were finishing the pot of chili, Grandpa asked, "Do any of you kids play cards?" They all answered in the affirmative.

"Good, I got a new game I just learned the other day when Danny and Mike Williams, from way up there at Le-Roy, came along with one of their politician friends and dropped by the cabin. I think that fellow was named Bill something; I know he was a republican, so, I banned all talking about politics. Fishing wasn't too good, so we got to playing cards. This new game is easy to learn and it's a lot

Grandpa Bern's Hotel

of fun. Course, with them three, I had to reinforce my rule against discussing politics, 'cause them three is all Republicans and I am a Democrat."

Woodie asked, "Who was the politician friend? It wasn't the Governor, was it?"

"Nah, that feller who was with the boys is a State Senator or Representative, I can't remember which. He had a real short name, but for the life of me, I can't recall it. Oh yeah, it was Bill Toot. Anyway he shore didn't like our Governor; he called her The Queen, and he was talking about some club he called 'The FAKers,' which he said meant, "Friends of Kathleen." I didn't think it was very funny; that's when I banned talking about politics."

The boys cleared the table and the girls washed the dishes. When they had finished putting everything away, Grandpa went for the cards. He came back with two decks of regular playing cards.

"Now, here is the rules to this game. First you take out the jokers and scuffle both decks together. Then the dealer, that'll be me the first time, passes out all the cards. That means, with six of us playing, everybody gets seventeen cards the first hand, with two sleepers left over. Now you arrange all your cards according to suits. You look them over and try to determine how many tricks you can take"

Sara asked, "Is there a trump?"

65

Carl Otto

"No, they ain't no trump. You have to follow suit if you got it, but you don't have to beat what's already down if you don't want to. Tricks is took according to the way they are in all card games, except pinochle. Ace is high, King next, then the Queen and so on down the line. But since we're playing with a double deck, they is two of each card. So if, for instance, somebody plays the King of spades, and then later another player tosses on the other King of spades, then the first one down is the boss. The way you figure your bid is, say for instance you got three aces. Well you know you can take at least three tricks if you can get in the lead."

Woodie asked, "What if you don't have any cards in a particular suit? Can you slough off a card in a different suit?"

"Oh yeah. The idée is to take the number of tricks you say your going take each hand. If you don't think you will take any trick atoll, you bid zero. The scorekeeper writes down all the bids at the beginning of each hand"

Jim asked, "What is the advantage of taking exactly what you bid?"

"Ah ha! That's the point. If you take exactly what you bid, you get what you bid plus a ten point bonus; if you go over what you bid, you get the number of tricks you took; but if you fail to reach your bid, you get your bid deducted from your score."

Kendra remarked, "So, you should try to bid exactly what you can take every hand; sounds like a good game."

Grandpa Bern's Hotel

"There is more to it. First hand you get seventeen cards; second hand you get sixteen, third hand you get fifteen, and so on down to the last hand when you get only one card."

Woodie inquired, "Then when the last hand is over, the person with the highest total is the winner?"

"No. The one with the lowest score is the winner. Nope, you're right. The one with the highest total is the winner – the highest total."

Bob asked, "I suppose you deal clockwise around the table, and then the person to your left deals the next hand."

"You got it. And we're all on our own. We don't have partners."

Bob asked, "What do you call this game?"

"Well, for tonight, we will call it, OH SHOOT. But that ain't what Danny Williams called it."

So the card game was under way by seven thirty. They took a break for coffee, milk and cookies at ten o'clock, but they resumed the game and played until well past midnight. Grandpa was the last one to say he was ready for bed. It had already been decided, while playing cards, what the sleeping arrangements would be. The boys would sleep upstairs in the west room; Woodie would sleep upstairs in the east room; the girls would sleep in the downstairs bedroom and grandpa would sleep where he usually sleeps, when he was not at the cabin – on a cot in his office.

Carl Otto

Grandpa's office was in a small room that had once been a nursery. He has a computer, on which he plays solitaire and other games, a desk, a TV, a file cabinet and an army cot sized bed. He also has what he called his "medicine cabinet." Grandpa is by no means a drinker, but he does keep a variety of "jugs," as he calls them. He has Peppermint Schnops, Vodka, Peach Brandy, Sweet Red Wine and Jack Daniels. He generally takes a little "nip" before bedtime each night. But he never takes more than his "nip."

He also has a locked steel gun cabinet where he keeps a double barreled 12 gauge shotgun, a 16 gauge pump action shotgun, a single barreled 410 gauge shotgun, a lever action 30.06 western style rifle, a 22 automatic rifle, a colt 45 revolver and holster, and a German Lugar he "borrowed" from a German officer during WWII.

He has said many times, "Oh dad gum it, I keep forgettin to return that Lugar to that Krout I borrowed it from."

The bottom drawer in that gun cabinet holds enough ammunition to fight off a good sized army. Whenever any of his family members complained about his arsenal he always says, "Oh, I aint got nothing compared to what some folks have. I don't ever plan on using any of it, but you never know."

By one o'clock, the kids had all excused themselves and gone on to bed. Grandpa Bern and his grandson stayed up another half hour visiting.

Grandpa Bern's Hotel

Finally the younger man said, "Grandpa, I cannot stay awake for another minute. I am hitting the sack."

He went on upstairs where he joined the chorus of snores coming from the adjoining bedroom; the boys were sound asleep.

As he settled in under the covers, he thought. "What a great evening. I'm glad this flood came along. I have met four refreshing young kids and I have enjoyed a fantastic evening with my grandpa. What more could anyone ask?"

True to historical instances in southeast Kansas, the next morning greeted everyone with a bright sun shining through a clear sky. The rainfall had ceased and was beginning to run off. The radio reports indicated a number of county road culverts had been washed out. The river was out of its banks and numerous roads were closed.

Woodie came down the stairs, as he smelled the coffee brewing.

"Mmmm, that smells good grandpa."

"I built a full pot. I can see the county crew headed this way. I expect they have the culverts replaced. You and the youngins ought to be able to get out of here before too long."

"Oh, I'm not leaving Grandpa, I'm going to spend a few days with you."

By ten o'clock James and Sara and Bob and Kendra were bidding Grandpa and Woodie farewell. They thanked

Carl Otto

grandpa and Woodie profusely; the girls even gave them both a big hug. As their vehicle was leaving the back yard, Grandpa turned to Woodie.

"You know something Woodie, them was four real fine youngins, but that little Kendra, — -well— --(cleared his throat) — she --ah – shore – she made me think — -of — - - your grandma Effie, — — — - when she was that age."

He pulled a big red hankie from his back pocket and blew his nose.

The weeks passed as life was progressing normally for old man Bern. He still spent as much time at his cabin as possible. But, he did keep in contact more frequently with Woodie and his other family members.

He came back to his house from the cabin one Wednesday afternoon and discovered James Bishop's car in his back yard. James and Sara were emerging from the front seat and Bob and Kendra were getting out of the back.

The four kids all rushed over to his pickup as he rolled to a stop.

"Dad gum it all, if you kids ain't a sight for sore eyes. What are you doing out here in the middle of the week on a school day? Are you playin hookey or are you selling magazines?"

Kendra was the first to speak up, "No grandpa, we're not selling anything. We came out here to make a special request of you."

Grandpa Bern's Hotel

He was thinking, "My gosh, if this kid, Kendra, asks me to fly to the moon, I'm afraid I'll have to give it a try."

He asked, "A special request? What kind of special request?"

Robert suggested, "Let's all go inside for a visit."

It was a happy reunion as the four youngsters and the old man walked to the house, chattering as they went. They visited a good half hour before grandpa's curiosity got the better of him.

"Let's get back to this "special request" you were talking about earlier."

Kendra spoke up. "First of all, we want to tell you that for the past five or six years, high school graduation has not been the same as it once was. We never have a speaker any more. The valedictorian and the salutatorian of the class each make a few remarks, the principal gets up and brags on everybody and then they hand out the diplomas. We want something different."

"Oh, is that right? How do I fit into this picture?"

Kendra added, "I am the valedictorian and James is the salutatorian. We have both decided we would like for you to speak to the class instead of us."

"ME! Make a speech! Oh kids, I ain't never made a speech in my life."

"Oh yes you have. We have checked up on you. You have talked to the County Commissioners a lot of times; you have

Carl Otto

talked to the Coop Board; you have talked at the Rural Water District meetings and you have talked at Fire Board."

"Yeah, but that ain't the same as talking to a Graduating Class."

Kendra said, "We don't care. We want you and we have told all the other kids about you. Will you do it?' Pleeeeeze?

When he looked into her eyes and saw his own Effie, he could not turn Kendra down. "Okay. I'll do it."

After a moment he added, "I will need one of them portable blackboards and a piece of chalk where I can write and draw something."

One month later it was high school graduation time. All the class members were seated in front of the stage. The program began with the principal introducing the valedictorian. Kendra stepped up behind the microphone.

"Good evening everybody. James and I have decided we are not going to speak tonight. Instead, we have asked Grandpa Woodrow Bern to say a few words. Would you come forward, Grandpa?"

Mr. Bern, dressed in his dark gray Sunday suit, white shirt and maroon tie, stood and came forward. Kendra started the applause as he walked up behind the podium.

"Thank you Kendra."

He continued, "I once heard a feller, by the name of George Ferguson, make a short speech in Kincaid, Kansas

Grandpa Bern's Hotel

to a bunch of youngins like you. He called his speech, TEN TWO LETTERED WORDS."

Without speaking another word, Mr. Bern stepped to the blackboard, picked up a piece of chalk, placed the short piece of chalk flat on the board so it would leave a wide mark and printed, in bold print, IF IT IS TO BE, IT IS TO BE ME.

He then stepped to the side of the blackboard so all could see what he had written.

"Now Graduates, I want you to think for a moment. What do them ten two lettered words tell you? If it is to be, it is to be me. I want every one of you to stare at them ten words until they are burned into your minds so you will never forget them.

"Now, I want each one of you to hold up your pointing finger."

He demonstrated, by holding up his own crooked pointing finger.

"Now point that finger at your own nose; hold it right there for a spell."

After a short pause, he continued, "As you go out into the world, or as you go on to further your education, who is it that has to be responsible for getting it done. You're right. It is you. When you point your own finger toward your own face, and you think, "Who am I pointing to?" Your answer is ME. Nobody else can do it, if it is going to have any mean-

Carl Otto

ing for you. You have to do it yourself. You can't blame anybody for any failure you have. So, my only advise to you, as you leave here tonight, is remember them ten two lettered words. IF IT IS TO BE, IT IS TO BE ME.

"Now I am gonna have you do what my friend Danny told me his politician friend once done when he talked to a graduating class. I want each and every one of you to stand by your chair."

All of the class members stood erect.

"Now turn around and raise the seat on that folding chair and see if there is anything under it."

A little noise and confusion went through the audience as the graduates each raised the seat of the chair on which they were sitting.

Grandpa continued, "Now take what you found under your chair and hold it up so the rest of the people can all see."

Nobody was aware that Grandpa had given the custodian a crisp new dollar bill for each graduate, and asked him to tape it under each graduates chair.

He continued, "All of you turn around and sit back down."

After they were all seated, Grandpa Bern added, "That little exercise was to teach you that you will never earn a dollar if you don't get up off your butt."

Grandpa Bern's Hotel

When the applause subsided, Grandpa said, "I have just one more thing to do. Kendra, Bob, Sara, and James, come on back up here with me."

He waited until he was flanked by the two couples before he continued. "Now Kids, let's all join hands. And, if you other graduates, as well as you folks in the audience want to foller suit, that'll be fine"

He waited another minute or two while nearly every person in the room began to stand and hold hands.

"Thank you. And now I know what I'm gonna do ain't politically correct, but I'm an old geezer who don't care what that other two percent thinks; I'm gonna say a prayer. Bow your heads, close your eyes, look up at the ceiling, or whatever you chose. Or, plug your ears, if you can't stand hearin a prayer."

After a short pause, he continued, "Lord, this is the future of our country standin here in this room tonite with these square hats on. And, I kin testify that if the rest of these youngins standin before you are anything like these four youngins up here with me, we don't have any worries. Lord, I ask you to put a special blessing on every one of them. And Lord, I want to go on record, in front of these fine folks this evening, when I say that I think the Ten Commandments ort to be plainly displayed in and on every public building in this land. We don't need any other laws; they say it all. Amen."

Carl Otto

Grandpa Bern's speech lasted a little more than ten minutes; the applause he received lasted well over ten minutes. Numerous individuals were heard remarking, "I will never forget that speech, in fact, I think it is the only one I have ever heard that is worth remembering."

When the applause finally subsided, James stepped to the microphone.

He said, "Thank you very much Grandpa. And, now I have a suggestion for all of my fellow graduates. I intend to take this dollar bill (he held it up and waved it around) and frame it. And in the frame, below the bill, will be written ten two lettered words. I think you should all follow my lead. Thank you."

James Bishop, Sara Jenkins, Bob Reynolds and Kendra Myers never forgot the night they spent in Grandpa Bern's hotel, nor did they ever forget those ten two lettered words, the dollar bill or the final admonition. They all followed James' advise, with some additions; the dollar bill has a black magic marker signature of Woodrow "Grandpa" Bern across the face, and the frame contains, directly below the dollar bill, the a picture of Grandpa, standing in front of his former house guests, as well as, IF IT IS TO BE IT IS TO BE ME.

THE END

Grandpa Bern's Hotel

HE WAS THERE

HE WAS THERE

Glenn D. Spergeon never knew either of his parents. His mother was a teenager who gave him up at birth and who never revealed the name of his father. For some unknown reason he was never adopted. So he was raised in a number of foster homes; he had no real family ties. He was starting his senior year of high school before he began to realize he had a chance in life. The only thing that kept him in high school was his athletic prowess; he had become an excellent football player, so his likely-hood of getting a full-ride athletic scholarship looked promising. He began to think that maybe he really could go to college, get a degree and then get a good job and make something of his life.

Glenn was thrilled beyond description when a prominent University offered him a full athletic scholarship to play football. He signed a letter of intent without hesitation, and, true to the Athletic Director's assessment of Glenn, he became one of the better athletes ever to play for that University. He was in his senior year of college; football season was over and he was concentrating on his final semester and making sure he had all the credits necessary for a degree, when the love bug bit him.

Glen is one of those individuals who went through his early years as a skinny, unattractive and backward child and

Carl Otto

through his early teen-age years with acne problems and an inferiority complex; however, by the time he was a senior in high school, things were much improved for him. He is one of those fortunate quirks of nature, considered a late bloomer, who suddenly and almost magically matured into a totally different person.

Glenn is five feet and eleven inches tall and he weighs one hundred eighty two pounds. He is considered by all of his friends as a downright handsome fellow. Because of his handsome face, his ideal body build and his athletic ability, as a high school student, college student and a young single man, he is considered to be one of the greatest catches on campus, by most of the young ladies his age; even though he never thought of himself as anything other than ordinary. And, he is actually shy and timid around the opposite sex.

And then, when he was no longer concentrating on football, he did begin to notice a certain girl seemed to be taking a special interest in him. As a matter of fact it was plain to others that this girl had "set her cap," so to speak, for Glenn. It was no surprise to the ones who had been observing when it was announced he and the daughter of a very prominent and wealthy family; a young lady who was a cheerleader and a homecoming queen, as well as the winner of several beauty contests, were getting married as soon as they graduated from college. Nor was it was a surprise to

Glenn's friends, even though most of them felt the girl was not really a very good choice.

Their wedding was one of the most elegant and expensive affairs ever to take place in Jenkins County, and the honeymooners were treated to a three-month round the world trip on a luxurious cruise ship. Everything was beyond Glenn's wildest dreams until, shortly after he and his bride returned home, she discovered she was pregnant; she was livid. She turned on Glenn like a rattlesnake. She wanted an abortion, but her mother, due to their self appointed elevated status in the community, assumed the position that the family could not take a chance on their friends discovering their daughter had an abortion. She suggested, indeed she insisted the young couple should spend a year in Europe, "to round out their educational experience." Her parents made arrangements for the young couple to move immediately into a Seaside Villa near Valencia, Spain to await the birth of their child.

Glenn's beautiful little "Barbie Doll," continued her new role as a first classed witch. He tried everything within his power to help her through the pregnancy, but she was a total basket case. Two months before the scheduled delivery date, she threw such a tantrum she ended up in the hospital emergency room. The doctor felt it advisable to take the baby by Cesarean Section.

Carl Otto

To make matters worse, the baby was born with Down Syndrome. Glenn's in-laws, especially his mother-in-law, immediately assumed the "misfortune" was due to defective genes of the father. She wanted to place the baby in a European Infant Care Facility and forget he was ever born.

Glenn finally took a stand. Remembering what a childhood he had gone through, he made up his mind that his son would have a father. He would not agree to a plan of abandoning the baby.

His position was, "You say he is Mongoloid because of me; I don't know and I don't care. I do know he is my son, and, I am not going to abandon him. I am going to raise him."

His wife was in such a confused mental state, that she allowed her parents, mostly her mother, to make all the decisions. Being young and overwhelmed, Glenn went along with most of their wishes.

Glenn's in-laws decided to have the marriage annulled and sign all parental rights over to the Glenn. He rented a room near the hospital so he could remain near his son until such time as the baby was strong enough to be released to his care. He had always been pretty much on his own, but now he found himself in a much different position. He was alone in a foreign country; he had no friends; he had no family, but he was strong and he was determined. And, fortunately, he had taken two years of Spanish while a high school student and two college classes in Spanish. He was not fluent, but he could get by and his language skills improved with every passing day. He was able to get a job as a Physical Therapist Assistant in the same hospital in which his son was being treated.

Much to Glenn's surprise, his ex father-in-law had the family lawyer contact him one day to inform him, unknown by the ex mother-in-law, he wanted to pay all the baby's hospital expenses, and Glenn's room and board, although the man never again personally contacted Glenn or saw the baby. When the baby was released, after a year of hospital and clinical care, the father-in-law again insisted, through his attorney, that Glenn take the baby, along with $50,000 in new one-hundred U. S. dollar bills, and never attempt to contact the mother or any of her family.

He was told by the attorney, that arrangements had been made for him to leave the baby with the institution they had discussed at the time the baby was born, if at any time he felt raising the child by himself was too much. Glenn never considered that option. He was determined to raise the boy himself.

Glenn was also given a telephone number and instructed that if or when he ever decided to return the baby to the States, to establish a residence and a bank account in a location no closer than five states away from New York, after which he was to call the number and read a coded message

Carl Otto

to the individual who answered the phone. Glenn could not understand exactly what they were implying, even though he did assume there would be further help for him and the boy, so he did keep the number and the note.

During the time while Glenn was waiting for his son to become strong enough to be released to his care, he became very strongly bonded with his child. He read every piece of literature he could find concerning Down Syndrome. He learned that in Great Brittan and in Europe, it is referred to as, Down's, while in the United States, it is called Down Syndrome. At one time there was a lady who advocated calling the condition, Up Syndrome. He learned from one of the doctors at the hospital of a new and very innovative facility in the U.S.A. located at Wheatridge, Colorado. The new facility was designed exclusively for the care, education and treatment of children with Down Syndrome.

Glenn became aware that for a woman as young as his wife, at the time of the baby's birth, the chances of her having a child with this condition were around one in fifteen hundred; and that chances increase as mothers are older. He learned that Down children seem to be more at risk for ear infections and other childhood diseases. And he learned their life expectancy is limited. So he is fully aware his devotion to his son is going to be tough, to say the least. However, he also knows there are many instances of Down Syndrome individuals finishing high school and even going

He Was There

on to get college degrees. With concentrated learning programs and loving and patient parents and teachers, it is still unknown what degree of success these individuals might obtain. Glenn remains optimistic.

Glenn made a promise to himself that he would learn more, and he would strive to see that his boy succeeded. He took his son back to the United States and moved to Wheatridge, Colorado. Since he did have adequate funds, for the time being, he rented an apartment and hired a babysitter while he began looking for a job.

His college major was in the field of Health and Physical Education, with minors in Science and in Mathematics. With his bi-lingual skills, he soon discovered he could easily secure a position as a middle school mathematics teacher of Hispanic students. He accepted the position and then phoned the number he had been given. A female voice answered the phone.

Glenn read the coded message to the woman. "Roses are red and sometimes white; I'm five states away and out of your sight."

The woman answered, "Excuse me Sir; would you mind repeating that."

"Roses are red and sometimes white; I'm five states away and out of your sight."

"Could you hold for a moment?"

"Yes, I will hold."

87

Carl Otto

A moment or so later, a man's voice answered, "This is Glenn, is it not?"

"Yes this is Glenn."

The man's voice continued. "You do not need to know who I am. This will be our only contact because the phone number you have just used will be discontinued as soon as we hang up.

"And?"

"First of all; where are you now located? I need to know you are at least five states away from New York."

"I am in Colorado."

"Fine. Now I am pleased to inform you that I am authorized to transfer a large sum of money to your bank account. You may use the money as you see fit; however, I suggest you first establish a trust fund for your son. You should have no problem finding someone at your bank to help you handle your account. Now, give me your account number and the location and name of your bank."

"Wait a minute. How do I know who you are? I am by no means wealthy, but I do have a reasonable amount of money in that account. I can't take a chance on losing any of it."

"Son, your ex father-in-law is a very wealthy man, and he wants to provide you with the financial security you will need to raise his grandson, even though he and the rest of his family have chosen to continue their lives as if you never existed and the boy was never born. I know you cannot ap-

He Was There

preciate their stance, but, rest assured, the boy's grandfather is considerably more compassionate than his wife or your ex-wife. As a matter of fact, neither of them is aware of this transaction, and your ex father-in-law insists it stay that way; However, with his vast holdings, he deserves no special accolades for this gesture. He can well afford it."

Glenn hesitated a moment, decided the man was sincere and then gave him the information he requested.

The man continued. "Go to your bank as soon as you have time and ask if there have been any transfers into your account. And, good luck Glenn. You are a much better person than any of your ex in-laws. Believe me, your life will be happier than it would have been as a member of that family."

"Thank you Sir."

Glenn hung the receiver on the cradle. He did not tell the man to whom he was just talking, that he was making the call from an unlisted phone in the office of one of his bank's vice presidents.

He turned to the vice president. "How long does it take to make a cash transfer from New York to Colorado?"

The man turned his chair around to his computer and began entering some information. He looked at the screen for a moment and then turned toward Glenn.

"Well Mr. Spurgeon, it looks like you have just become a millionaire."

Carl Otto

"Are you serious? Let me take a look at that screen."

"There it is. Your account shows a balance of one million, twenty-seven thousand, six hundred seventy-two dollars and sixteen cents."

All Glenn could say was, "WOW!"

The vice president is the son of the bank's president and is not many years older than Glenn. His name is Richard Warner Jr.

Richard said, "Your expression indicates this transfer of money is a surprise to you."

"It most certainly is. I would not have been surprised at 50 thousand or so, but a million dollars - - Wow!"

Richard extended his hand, "Congratulations, Glenn; it looks like your financial worries, if you had any, are over. And, if you need a financial advisor, I would be happy to do it for you."

"I am certainly going to need an advisor. Do you know how much of that money I can keep and how much I will have to give to the tax collector?"

"The transfer code numbers indicate the entire amount is tax free. Your benefactor has taken care of that. You will, however, have to pay tax on the earnings this amount of money will generate."

"I have an toddler son who has Down Syndrome. The money is from his wealthy maternal grandfather. My ex-wife's family thought it was my fault that the boy had Downs, but it is apparent my ex-father-in-law wishes to provide the funds to raise the child. So, I want to establish a trust fund for him, and, I want to enroll my son in a Down Syndrome program as soon as possible. I would like to put the rest into investments. Could I hire you to do all that for me?"

"No, you can't hire me. I am your banker. That is a part of our services. So, other than the regular established fees, there is no charge for handling your money. With an account as large as yours, we will do okay. I can handle your money, but you will have to take care of enrolling your child in that school. How much do you want left in your checking account?"

"What would you suggest?"

Richard answered, "Let's see; the record shows you already had a little over four thousand in a checking account and a substantial sum in a savings account Why don't we just leave the present checking account as is, and temporarily place all the rest of the money in an open savings account. I will set up a trust fund and look into stable investments, after which, I will call you in for a conference to get your approval of everything. How does that sound?"

"Great. Richard, I am trusting you to take care of everything."

"I will. And you rest assured that your money is safe with us, and you are in charge of it. If at any time you wish to transfer more to your checking account or if it ever happens that you are overdrawn, we will automatically make a transfer to your checking account. You just let me know of any change you want to make."

Glenn was still reeling from the shock of what he had just experienced as he left the bank and started for his car. He was thinking, "I guess my ex father-in-law is a much better man than I have given him credit. Now, I will have the funds to put my boy in a good training facility."

Little David Glenn Spurgeon weighed a mere 4 pounds 8 ounces when he was born, but in spite of being delivered early, he is healthier than most babies with his condition. He seems to be a happy baby, at least he appears that way to his young father. The boy does exhibit most of the characteristic signs of the condition; however, none are extreme. He does have the oval shaped eyes, the shortened arms and legs; the stubbier fingers and the single crease in the palms of his hands, but to a casual observer, he might not be recognized as a Down child.

Glenn checked out a newspaper add as soon as he arrived in Wheatland, in which an elderly woman listed a room in her home. He drove there and visited with the old lady about the room and the possibility of hiring her as a baby sitter. Mrs. Elsie Davenport is a 64 year-old widow who is living on a fixed income, so the $1000.00 monthly rent and babysitting fee they agreed upon is great for her as

He Was There

well as being a Godsend for Glenn. Elsie prefers to be called Granny, and she is an unbelievably great baby sitter.

After discovering he was now a millionaire, Glenn wondered if he might be taking advantage of Mrs. Davenport; however, since he was still unaware of what it would cost to have David enrolled in such a sophisticated special education program, he kept his financial status to himself.

It was August 1 when Glenn had a contract in hand to begin teaching the English language and mathematics to Hispanic students at the local Middle School. He still had plenty of time to check out a pre-school educational program for David, who is now sixteen months old. So, with all financial worries behind him, things seemed to be falling into place for Glenn and David.

Glenn parked his car in the parking lot of the Down Syndrome facility he wanted to investigate. He is not an extremely religious person; but, before he got out of his car, for some reason, he looked up, closed his eyes and said, "Lord, if you can hear me and are interested in me and my little boy, could you please make this visit to this school a positive beginning and an answer to my problem?"

He then got out of his car and started walking toward the side entrance of the building. As he walked past an old beat up car in one of the parking places, he noticed what appeared to be a girl or a small woman leaning her head on folded arms on the steering wheel; she was sobbing.

Carl Otto

Glenn stopped by her driver's side door and asked, "Are you alright?"

The young woman jerked and looked up from her bent over position. She burst into uncontrollable crying. Glenn did not know what to do, but he instinctively knew this young woman needed help. He reached in the open window and placed a hand or her shoulder.

"I'm sorry. I didn't mean to frighten you. Is there anything I can do for you?"

Through her sobbing, she answered, "Oh, -- I don't know — that — anyone — can do anything for me — I am at my wits end."

"I don't know whether I can help you or not, but you need somebody to try."

Trying to stop crying, she said, "A person who has - - - - - has never cared — - for a child — - with, with, with Down Syndrome - - - - could have no idea what, what, ah what I'm

He Was There

– I'm – I'm - going through."

"Well, guess what? Little Lady. You are looking at the father of a Down Syndrome child. I think I might understand fully what you are going through."

She stopped crying and looked up at Glenn, "No kidding? You too?"

Glenn looked into her big brown eyes and he was suddenly consumed with a feeling he could not describe. He was thinking, "I have finally found someone who understands my situation."

After a short pause, he said, "My name is Glenn. What is yours?"

"Sara."

"Well Sara, I have some free time. Would you allow me to buy you a cup of coffee? There is a Café, right across the street."

She sighed deeply and answered, "I -- I --I would love to have a cup of coffee."

Glenn opened the driver's door and extended his hand to Sara. When she stepped out of the car and stood erect, he could see she was a very disheveled individual; she was more than a head shorter than Glenn. Her clothing was clean, but obviously old; her head passed close to his face when she got out of her car; her hair was clean an free of any odor; she wore no make up and her nails were clean but unpainted.

Carl Otto

From the looks of her old car, it was obvious this young lady probably was having financial problems.

They walked across the street and entered the Café without talking. As they sat down in a booth, Glenn looked at his watch. "Well, it is now 11:17 a.m. I believe I could eat an early lunch. Do you have time to eat lunch with me, Sara?"

She started to say something, but Glenn cut her off. "Don't answer. I insist. I am hungry, and I am tired of eating alone. I want to buy your lunch."

Sara smiled and pushed her hair back. "Okay, if you insist. I really am hungry."

A waitress was now standing by the booth. She asked, "Are you two ready to order your drinks now?"

Glenn ordered coffee and water and Sara ordered a glass of milk. The waitress handed them menus.

She said, "I'll be back in a moment to take your orders."

Glenn said, "I don't know about you Sara, but I am going to get a steak."

Glenn continued, "That's one thing good about having an expense account; I can eat steak, and I can buy a steak dinner for a client. And my boss just loves to pay for them."

"Are you serious?"

"Yes I'm serious. Order the biggest steak in the house if you want it. My boss doesn't care."

"Oh my, I haven't had a steak in so long, I can't remember when I did."

He Was There

"Well, then that is settled. We will have steak."

All the while they were ordering, Glen was observing this little woman closely. He was thinking, "She looks like she is about my age. She does have pretty brown eyes. She has a nice smile and a pleasant sounding voice; and, I'll bet her hair could be fixed to look real nice. My, she is so thin. I'll bet she doesn't weigh ninety pounds."

Sara was thinking, "My this fellow is a nice looking man. He says he is the father of a Downs child. He looks like he must be thirty-five. I wonder if his wife is older than him. He sounds sincere about his expense account. Anyway he has asked me to have lunch with him, and I am hungry."

There was no doubt about Sara being hungry. She ate a big baked potato with sour cream, and she slicked up every morsel of salad and green beans as well as the ten once steak and a big glass of milk, with a refill.

With her tummy filled, Sara sat back and relaxed. "Do you want to know why I was crying?"

"If you want to tell me, yes, I am interested."

"Well, you see, my little girl is with a friend, while I went to that building across the street to find out what is involved in enrolling her in their program. But, I found there is no way I can even begin to pay the fees."

"Well, guess what, Sara? That is the reason I was in that parking lot today."

Carl Otto

Sara sat up straight, as she answered, "How old is your child?"

"He is sixteen months old. How old is your child?"

"She is fifteen months old."

Glenn leaned back. "Well, Sara, it looks like we definitely have something in common. Where is your husband?"

"My husband left me as soon as he realized Patty was a Downs child. He blamed my side of the family. He joined the Navy, and I have not heard from him since he left."

"Are you still married to him?"

"I don't know. I could never afford a lawyer to get a divorce. And, if he ever bothered to divorce me, I have never been informed."

"Do you have a job?"

"The only job I could find, where I am allowed to take my baby to work with me, is working for a house cleaning service. I get paid $5.00 an hour when I work."

Glenn thought, "Five dollars and hour. My Lord how can she get buy?"

He continued, "I'll bet you don't have health insurance, do you?"

"I don't have any kind of insurance."

"You don't have vehicle insurance?"

"I barely make enough money to buy food and gasoline. I don't even have a car seat for Patty. And, I'm scared to death I am going to get a ticket some time."

He Was There

"Where do you live?"

"Right now, I am living with a friend, but I know her husband doesn't want us with them, so sometimes we just stay in my car."

Glenn was just bowled over. "Oh my, Sara. You can't live like that with a baby."

"I don't have any choice."

"Don't you have a family?'

"No. I was raised by several pairs of foster parents until I was sixteen; I have been on my own since then."

Glenn sat and pondered the situation for a moment. He was thinking, "Oh Lord, what would I do if I were in her place?"

Sara started to get up to leave. Glenn reached across and took her by the arm.

"Wait. Let me think awhile. Maybe I can help you."

She sat back down. "You don't know a thing about me. Why would you try to help me?"

"Because I too, was once abandoned. I too was raised in foster homes, and now I have been abandoned again; this time with a child. My wife and her people blamed the child's condition on me; I too was told my son was like he is because of my family background. Her parents had our marriage annulled and gave me full legal rights to my son. I know what it is to try to raise a baby by yourself."

"What will you do?"

Carl Otto

"I don't know right now. But first, let's go back across the street to my car and talk."

Glenn paid the check for their meal and they walked back across the street to his car. They both entered his car and shut the doors. Glenn sat for a full minute before he said, "Sara, this might sound like the craziest proposal you have ever heard, and it could well be just that, but I have an idea I would like to run by you."

"Okay, tell me about it; I'm desperate."

"What would you think about an arrangement whereby I would pay all the living expenses and you would help take care of my boy?"

"Just what are you getting at?"

"I mean, what if I would pay for all expenses in sending your little girl to that special Down school; I will buy health insurance for you both; I will pay all room and board expenses as well as other expenses, and you would take care of and accompany both babies to the special school. They do encourage parents to accompany the kids and help with the special training, you know."

Sara was flabbergasted. She didn't know what to say.

Glenn continued, "I have a good job as a school teacher. I have to report for in service training within two weeks of today. So, I need to get my family arrangements done right away. What do you think?"

He Was There

"You're a school teacher? Then you don't have a boss that just 'loves' to pay for 'client' dinners, do you?"

"Well, no I don't. I fibbed a little; I didn't want you to feel embarrassed or anything."

"I guess I probably wouldn't have let you buy my lunch if you hadn't fibbed to me."

"Well, what do you say about my proposition?

Sara was still shaking her head in amazement. "Now let me get this straight? You are telling me that you will pay the tuition for my baby to attend this school; that you will pay for health insurance and other expenses for me and my baby; that you will pay for room and board for me and my baby, and all I have to do is stay at home and take care of the two babies and accompany them to this special school."

"That is exactly what I am proposing. You would have to discontinue your present job; your job would be full time taking care of the babies. Of course, I will help when I am home, and I will still hire a baby sitter to also help. I will also provide you with the cash allowance you'll need for personal things. I will pay all other expenses"

"You can't make enough as a teacher to do all that?"

"No I can't, but I have some money saved."

"How can I be sure you are not pulling my leg?"

"Sara, I have to admit, I have a selfish motive here. I cannot accompany David to the school because I will be working. I have a feeling I can trust you because we are in the

Carl Otto

same boat. And I am financially independent, so I can afford it. Now, how about it?"

Sara started several times to open her mouth as if to say something before she finally said, "I simply cannot believe anyone would put that much trust in a complete stranger, but I also cannot believe anyone with any brains at all would turn down an offer like this one. I think if you are really serious, I am willing to try."

Glenn extended his hand. "Let's shake on it."

Glenn added, "Now, to prove to you I am not pulling your leg, the first thing we will do is go in that building and enroll the kids in that special school. Then we will go to Granny's and make sure she has room for you. If she does not, we will rent a house or an apartment. Then we will go get your baby and your stuff and get the ball rolling."

"Is this Granny your grandmother?"

"No, she is the lady who owns the house where I stay. She is also David's baby sitter. I know she has another room, and I have a feeling she will rent it."

"What will I do about my old car?"

"We will take care of it later."

Glen exited the car on the driver side while Sara got out on the other side. They met in front of the car where Glenn asked, "What is your last name?"

"Pershing. That is my maiden name; my married name is Jones, but I am taking my maiden name back."

He Was There

"My name is Glenn Spurgeon."

"Okay, Glenn Spurgeon, you're the boss."

Glenn stopped and turned toward Sara. "No Sara, I am not the boss. We are partners in this venture. You will be earning your keep."

This time she stopped. "Just what do you mean by that?"

He looked down at her small thin frame. "Sara, I am an honorable man. I do not intend to take advantage of you in any way. I promise you that you will never be asked to do anything you do not approve of doing. Okay?"

"Okay. I don't understand why, but I believe you."

Sara was thinking, "Oh Lord, I must be dreaming. Surely this cannot actually be happening. But somehow, I have a feeling this man is exactly what he says."

They went into the building and started the process of getting the children enrolled in the program. With the paper work finished, Glenn wrote a check for the full year of services for both children. When they went out the door, Glenn said, "Now. Your child is enrolled for a year no matter what we agree to do from this point on."

The next stop was at Mrs. Davenport's. David is just now beginning to walk by himself without help. He toddled over to meet his daddy as Sara and he entered the front door. Glenn picked him up and hugged and kissed him.

Then he turned to Mrs. Davenport. "Granny, I know you have another room. This young lady, Sara Pershing, also

103

Carl Otto

has a Down Syndrome child. We met at the school and we have reached an agreement and have made an arrangement whereby she will help take care of David, and she would also accompany both children to the special school. Is it possible that she might move into your other spare room?"

Granny looked Sara up and down for a moment. "Of course we have room for you and your little girl." She held out her arms and Sara went to her for a hug.

Glenn said, "I will pay you an additional thousand dollars a month. But, you do understand the deal is, Sara will stay here with you and help take care of the kids. She will also be accompanying them to their special school. Do you think you can handle that Granny?"

Granny added, "My Lord Glenn, that would be two thousand dollars a month. Can you afford that on a teachers salary?"

"Well, I have other funds available too. Then is it a deal?"

"It's a deal. When are you moving in, Sara?"

Glenn answered, "As soon as we can go get Patty and Sara's stuff."

Suddenly Sara was overcome with emotion. She went to a chair and wilted down; holding her face in her hands, she began to cry. Through shaking sobs, she said, "I don't know what to say.— I just cannot believe — this is actually happening. I have worked so hard to get by.— And now it seems — my troubles are suddenly over."

104

He Was There

Glenn went the Sara, knelt down on one knee and put one hand on her shoulder. "I know this is all happening so quickly. I understand how unbelievable it seems to you. It seems unbelievable to me too. I never, in my wildest dreams, would have thought I would find someone like you who could help me with my problem."

Sara threw both arms around Glenn's neck and held him tightly. "You are an Angel; that's what you are; an Angel. There is no other way of describing how I feel."

Glenn stood up and pulled Sara up with him. He held her in his arms with his chin resting on top of her head as tears welled up in his own eyes. "It's going to be alright, Sara. It's going to be alright. We may be total strangers now, but we are going to make this thing work.

Little David was tugging at Glenn's leg. He bent over and picked David up.

"David, this is Sara."

David looked at Sara through those oval eyes, and then extended his chubby hands out to her. She took him into her arms and kissed him. "Hi David. I can't wait for you to meet my little Patty."

Glenn added, "I can't wait to meet her either; let's go get her."

While they were driving across town to get Sara's daughter and her things, Glenn told her about his former wife and how the marriage ended. He didn't tell her the amount, but

Carl Otto

he did tell her his ex father-in-law had provided funds for the care of David.

He told her, "You will not have to worry about money anymore; I have enough for both of us."

Upon arriving at the house of Sara's friend, Glenn and Sara were greeted by an irate young man and a young woman. The woman was crying.

The man said, "Sara, I hate to tell you this, but you can no longer live here. I just cannot stand looking at that kid of yours one minute longer."

Glenn stepped forward. "You won't have to look at that kid of hers any longer. She has found someone who will enjoy looking at her kid. We have come to get Sara's things and the baby."

Suddenly the man's demeanor changed. He said, "I'm sorry. I should not have said that, Sara. I really didn't mean it."

Sara answered, "It's okay Jim, I don't blame you. I am indebted to you for allowing me to stay here as long as you did."

Sara's friend spoke up, "Sara, who is this guy?"

Glenn answered before Sara could speak. "We are old friends. We met at a school for Down Syndrome children. You see I am also the parent of one of these beautiful children. Sara and I have decided we can provide better care for our kids if we do it together. She will be living with me."

He Was There

"Are you two going to get married?"

Sara answered, "Mary, you know I am still married."

"Not any more. I took the liberty of opening this letter from a law firm you received today. Here read this."

Sara took the letter from Mary and began reading. After a moment she handed it to Glenn. He looked at the letter for a moment.

"Well Sara, it looks like you are a free woman again."

Mary added, "Then you two are getting married?"

Glenn answered, "That subject has not been discussed. We will table it for now."

Thirty minutes later, Glenn, Sara and little Patty, along with a highchair and two suitcases of her belongings, were loaded into Glenn's car and were headed for Granny's. Patty was securely fastened in David's car seat. Sara was so happy she was giddy. She giggled and laughed at everything.

Glenn was thinking, "It is amazing what a laugh and positive attitude can do for a person. Sara is thin, but she is downright pretty."

Glenn asked, "How old are you Sara?"

"I'm almost nineteen."

"You are only eighteen years old?"

"I'll be nineteen in two months."

"My gosh, I figured you were younger than me, but —

"I know. I look like I'm thirty. I'm so skinny and beat up. How old did you think I was?"

Carl Otto

"Well, until a short while ago, when you began to laugh, I did think you were older. But, I can now see that you are much younger than me."

"How old are you?"

"How old would you guess me to be?"

"Oh gosh, let's see. I think you must be like, thirty-five."

Glenn began to laugh. "Thirty-five! How about that?"

"Well, how old are you?"

"I'm twenty-four."

Her mouth dropped open and she looked shocked. "You're just twenty-four years old. Wow!"

"Sara, I guess trying to raise a special child by yourself, like we have been doing; kind of wears on a person, doesn't it."

Sara reached over and placed her hand on Glenn's right shoulder. "I'm sorry I guessed you at thirty-five; are you sure you still want to go ahead with this arrangement? You are taking on quite a responsibility for a young guy."

He reached up and placed his right hand over hers. "We have both been through the mill. Our experience has probably aged us beyond our actual years, but we now have found each other. And, yes, I am sure I want to go ahead with this arrangement. In fact, I feel better right now than I have since before my ex wife knew she was pregnant"

"I am positive I want to go on with it. I sure don't have anything to lose. As a matter of fact, Glenn, I haven't known you twenty-four hours, but already I love you. I can't believe there is man in the whole world who could come close to being as nice and as generous as you."

He squeezed her hand, but said nothing, as he continued driving along for several more blocks. He was thinking, "I wish I would have met Sara before I met Bridget. She says she already loves me, and I don't think it would be very hard for me to learn to love her."

He continued to drive and think. "Getting family health insurance would be a lot simpler if Sara and I did get married."

Suddenly he pulled off the street and parked in a parallel parking spot. He turned to Sara and said. "Sara, I know this sounds crazy, but what would you think about making this whole arrangement legal and permanent?"

"Exactly, what are you saying?"

"I am saying, let's you and I get married. You are free now. We are both young, and we both have our physical needs as well as our mutual problems."

"You can't be serious?"

"Sara, I dated my wife for five months before we got married. I thought I knew her, but I didn't have the faintest idea of who she really was. I think I already know more about you, and see more good in you than I ever did in her. And besides you just said you already love me."

Carl Otto

She answered, "Huh, I guess I can say the same thing about the guy I married. I really did not know what kind of person he was until Patty was born. Then came the true test. And, yes, I did say I already love you."

Glenn continued, "If we were married, I think the entire arrangement would be much less complicated."

"Glenn, you are really a good looking guy; you could probably have most any woman you wanted. I, on the other hand, am a Plain Jane. I don't even have a high school education and you're a teacher. Do you really think you could learn to love me?"

"Oh Sara, You are not a Plain Jane; you have beautiful brown eyes; you have a very pleasant smile; I love to hear you laugh; you are sensitive and forgiving. And, as for your education; you are only eighteen, there is still plenty of time for that"

"How do you know I am forgiving?"

"I think most women would have scratched Jim's eyes out back there, when he made that remark about Patty. But you were actually forgiving."

"I knew he really didn't mean it."

"Sara, you say you were raised in foster homes; I too was raised in foster homes; you say you were married to a person who blamed you because your baby was not perfect; I too was married to a person who blamed me; you have been struggling and worrying ever since Patty was born; I have

He Was There

not had the financial worries you have had, but I too have been struggling and worrying ever since David was born. Good gravy Sara, how could two people be more suited for one another?"

"When you put it that way, I guess we are a pretty good match."

"Scoot over here close to me."

She unfastened her seatbelt and slid over to Glenn. He put his arms around her slim body, and held her tightly.

Through a stream of tears, Sara answered, "Oh Glenn, I know I have died and gone to heaven. Nobody but an angel could be this good to me."

They sat and held each other for a full minute before Glenn added, "Sara, I cannot explain how good I feel right now. I know this sounds crazy, but somehow I feel pushed toward you like we are the only two people in the world with such need for each other. I think I must have loved you before I ever saw you. Yes, I know I did, I love you too Sara, and I need you; oh how I need you. I want you to be my wife. What do you say?

She answered, "Oh, Glenn, this is so overwhelming. My mind is in a whirl. I don't know what to say."

"You don't have to answer right now; just think about it. Now, put your seatbelt back on, and we'll go to Granny's."

Sara slid over and began to fasten her seatbelt as she said, "I hope you really do need me as much as I need you,

Carl Otto

because, Lord only knows, I do need somebody like you."

They first took little Patty in the house and placed her on the floor in front of David. The two children just stared at each other for a long moment, and then they both began to smile big smiles. David crawled over to Patty and put his little arms around her. Both children toppled over and Patty began to cry. Sara picked her up and Glenn picked David up. They held the two children facing each other.

Granny said, "They will get used to each other. I think I bawled the first time I ever saw my late husband."

Sara and Glenn laughed.

Granny continued, "I'm sure he bawled when he saw me."

Sara put Patty down and hugged Granny. "I can see it is going to be great living here."

He Was There

It didn't take long to unload Sara and Patty's belongings; they did not have much. And, by the time Glenn and Sara had made two trips back and forth between the house and the car, Granny had the two children playing in the middle of the floor.

The one thing Sara did have was a good high chair for Patty, so when it came feeding time, they placed the two kids in their high chairs side by side. Both kids were ready for a nap as soon as they were fed.

With the children sleeping, Glenn said, "Granny, do you think you can handle the situation while we go get Sara's car?"

Granny answered, "If Patty sleeps as well as David, you will have plenty of time."

Sara responded, "Oh, she does, when she is feeling well, and she is over her cold now. She will probably sleep at least two hours, then as soon as she is fed and changed, she will be down for the night."

David said, "How about that. Looks like the kids have similar sleeping patterns."

He continued, "Granny, we might take a little longer. I want to stop at that health food store and get more of those special vitamins and minerals, and we need to buy another car seat. Is there anything else we need to get?"

Carl Otto

"I don't know of anything Glenn. I think you have a pretty good supply of everything. You two go ahead, and don't worry about the kids; I have that situation well in hand."

Glenn hugged Granny and said, "You're a doll, Granny."

"Oh, poof. Get out of here."

Once out in the car, Glenn said, "We don't have time to do it now, but our next move is to get you a better car. Do you have the title to that one?"

Sara got a puzzled look.

Glenn continued, "Sara, you don't have a title, do you?"

"No. The car isn't even registered."

"Sara! How long have you been driving that car with no registration? You do have a driver's license, surely."

"Yes, I have a driver's license. I've had the car about a year. I bought it from a high school kid for a hundred ninety-two dollars."

"Did you know anything about the kid?"

"No. I saw the car sitting on the street with a for sale sign on it. So I walked over and started looking at it. Then this kid showed up and said it was his. He said it had been a wreck and he fixed it up, but he didn't have a title."

"I'll bet he wanted cash, didn't he?"

"He wanted three hundred, but when I told him I had been saving for over a year and all I had was one hundred ninety-two. He told me since I looked like I really needed a car he would make me a good deal."

114

He Was There

"He probably told you he had been driving it for a long time and had never even been stopped."

"Yes, he said if you obey all the rules and don't speed, the cops never stop you."

"Holy cow, it could be a stolen car!"

She answered, "I asked him if it was, but he assured me it wasn't. He just didn't have a title."

Sara started crying. "Oh, what have I done? Am I going to get in trouble?"

"Don't cry. I'll take care of everything."

"What are you going to do?"

"Just don't you worry. I will take care of it."

They drove along in silence as Glenn reached over to squeeze her folded hands while he pondered the situation. By the time they reached the parking lot where she left her car, someone else had solved the problem; her car was gone.

She sat up straight and placed her hands to her mouth.

"Sara, did you leave anything in that car that would tie you to it?"

"No. I never left anything in it because I couldn't lock it. I never did have a key for it and it didn't even need a key to start it."

"It didn't need an ignition key?"

"No. All I had to do is twist where the key is supposed to go."

Carl Otto

"No kidding!"

"Yeah, that's right. I had to be careful not to lock the doors. I did that once and Jim had to take a clothes hanger to open it."

Glenn added, "Well, I am sure it has been stolen, because it has not been here long enough to have been towed away."

She looked at Glenn with tears in those big brown eyes. "What am I going to do?"

"Come over here to me."

She slid over to Glenn and he put his arms around her.

"We are going to act like that old wreck never existed. We are going to the next dealership we come across and buy you a good car."

"Glenn, you can't keep doing things like that — ."

He put a finger up to her lips.

"Shush. Yes I can, and I will. No further discussion. But first we go get that car seat."

"Oh my Glenn, what would I do if I hadn't run into you."

"The point is we ran into each other. I need you as bad as you need me."

"I don't know how anyone could be in more need than me."

He said, "That's beside the point; let's think about that car seat now."

Sara said, "They have a good one that I have been looking at in Wal Mart."

116

He Was There

"Good enough. That is where we will go."

He took her face in his two hands and kissed her on the corner of her mouth.

"Now, get back in your seatbelt; we're headed for Wal Mart."

After purchasing a good car seat, the next stop was at a Toyota dealership. They looked at several models before Glenn settled on a steel gray 2005 Camry LE. Sara thought it was much too expensive, but Glenn insisted she needed a good reliable car in which to transport the kids.

He told the salesman, "Okay, we like this one. Take twenty percent off that sticker price and I'll write you a check for it."

"Don't you want to take it for a test drive?"

"Nope. I already have one about like it. I know how they are. And besides, it has a thirty day warranty; if there is anything wrong, we'll soon find out."

The salesman hesitated a moment and then said, "I can't reduce the price that much."

Glenn answered, "Is that right? Well, I tell you what. It has been nice visiting with you. Come on Sara, let's go get that other one we looked at."

"Wait a moment. You say you want to pay cash?"

"With a check. I want to buy it outright."

Carl Otto

The salesman looked surprised, but happy. "Okay. Twenty percent it is. Come on in and we will do the paper work. How do you want it titled?"

"I want it titled to Glenn D Spurgeon and/or Sara S. Spurgeon."

She tugged at his arm and whispered, "I'm not a Spurgeon yet."

He whispered back, "Oh that's right. You haven't said yes yet. Holy Cow, now what are we going to do?"

She whispered, "I guess I'll have to say yes."

He leaned close to her, "What was that again?"

"I said yes, I will marry you."

"Great! We'll drive down to Oklahoma tomorrow and tie the not."

He told the sales person. "I'll pay for it now; you get it ready, we will be in tomorrow morning to pick it up."

As they were leaving, Sara asked, "How did you know my middle initial was S?"

"I guess I am just psychic."

"You're not either. How did you know?"

"I saw that letter from your ex-husband's lawyer was addressed to Sara Sue Jones."

"How did you know that salesman would reduce the price of that car twenty percent?"

"I didn't know. I have always heard they could, so I decided to run a bluff."

He Was There

When they got back in the car to go back to Granny's, Sara said, "Glenn, you said you have plenty of money. Are you sure you're not getting yourself into financial trouble? You are spending a lot of money."

"Don't worry about it. I'll take care of that end."

"But I do worry about it. I think if I am going to agree to this marriage thing, I should be told everything."

He hesitated a moment before answering, "You're right Sara; you do deserve to hear everything. I was going to wait until after we were married, but somehow, I don't think my money had a thing to do with your decision. I think you would have agreed to marry me and go into this child raising partnership, even if I were penniless."

"I really think I would. I have been struggling alone, thinking I was the only person in the world with my problem. Then you came along and I find I am not alone. I just feel like I have always known you."

She hesitated a moment before she continued, "Now I suppose you're going to tell me you are a millionaire, or something like that."

He chuckled, "That is exactly what I am going to tell you."

"You are saying that you are a millionaire?"

"Yes, I am a millionaire."

"Oh bull! A young guy like you; you would have to come from a rich family?"

Carl Otto

"No I don't come from a rich family, I am just what I have told you I am, but I am a millionaire. My ex father-in-law, at the time my ex wife and her family decided they wanted nothing to do with David, first gave me fifty thousand dollars to help take care of him. He told me, when I came back to the United States, to call a certain number as soon as I established a residence that was located at least five States away from New York, and read a coded message. When I did that, he had his lawyer transfer a cool million dollars to my bank account."

"Oh my goodness! Really? Then you really are a millionaire? You really are?"

He nodded his head yes as she talked.

"And you still intend to go ahead with what we have planned?"

"Yes, I am, and yes I do."

She sputtered, "Ah – well - ah – ah - do you want me to sign one of those pre-getting married things?"

"Hmm, I never thought about that. But, you know what? That money came to me out of the blue, and I would not have it if I were not the father of a Down child. And, I would never have found you, if you had not been a parent of a Down child. I think we are destined to be a family together. So, I will just share it with you. I cannot believe anyone could be more deserving. And, maybe, by working together,

He Was There

we can use that money to make sure our two special children will have a fighting chance in this world."

Sara sat silently for a moment before she said, "Glenn, do you believe in God?"

He thought for a moment before her answered, "There was a time when I questioned the existence of God; however, when I stopped to take a good look at the whole picture, I came to believe there has to be a Supreme Power. At first, I blamed God for allowing a handicapped child to be born, but then I reasoned that an all-powerful entity, even as powerful as God, can't stop some unpleasant things from happening. If everything in the world was pleasant, I think we would get tired of pleasant."

She looked at Glenn and answered, "You know what? I have sat holding Patty, when she was sick, and looked up and cursed God. There have been times when I was almost to the point of drowning myself and her along with me."

Glenn reached over and patted her hand. "I know, I know."

"And then one late cold windy night, a few months ago, when Patty was crying and crying, I took her out to my car because I didn't want to disturb Jim. I just wrapped up in a big old quilt and held her close in my arms.

And, as I sat there shivering, I looked up and said, 'Dear God, if you are there, and you can hear me; please; please; please help me before I just lose it all and do something bad.'

Carl Otto

Suddenly, Patty stopped crying, and I had a warm feeling come over my entire body and the air all around me got real warm. I never heard a thing but we were not cold and Patty was not crying; it was only a feeling, but Patty went to sleep. I leaned the seat back and dozed off myself, with her on my belly, and I didn't wake up until morning."

"Wow! Do you really think God was answering your prayer?"

"Yes, I think He did. I have never told anybody about it until right now, because I thought somebody might think I was nuts or something."

"It's alright. That was just between you and God. You didn't need to tell anyone."

"There is more, Glenn. When you first found me leaning on my steering wheel and crying, I was saying to myself, 'Oh God, why me? What have I done to deserve all this trouble? Am I completely forsaken?' I wasn't really praying; I was just talking to myself. And then you appeared."

Glenn suddenly remembered that before he got out of his car, he had closed his eyes and said a short prayer.

He said, "I swear I am not making this up, Sara. And you might not believe this, but at the same time you were leaning on that steering wheel, I was closing my eyes, looking up and asking God to make my visit to that school an answer to my problem."

He Was There

She just looked at Glenn with an expression of total wonderment.

He continued, "Religious people say that God knows all, sees all and hears all. Maybe He heard us both and decided we were destined to be together. All I can say is; if we are destined to be together, I am satisfied with the arrangement."

She looked intently at Glenn and said, "He was there!"

Glenn answered, "Yes Sara, He was there. God really was there."

Glenn drove his car into the driveway beside Granny's house, stopped and turned off the ignition.

Sara said, "May I kiss you, Glenn?"

"I really think you should. Come here."

She unfastened her belt and literally jumped up in the seat on her knees and threw both arms around Glenn. Hugging him tightly, she said, "Oh thank you Lord. Thank you Lord. I just know you had something to do with all this.

THE END

WHATEVER HAPPENED TO ELMER

WHATEVER HAPPENED TO ELMER

Sheriff Milton Mayberry decided it was time he got a haircut, so he told his deputy where he was going and headed down the street to the barbershop.

As he entered the shop, the barber said, "Mornin Sheriff, how ya doin?"

"Oh, if I were any better, I couldn't stand it. How you doin?"

"Well, I'm still in the Hair today gone tomorrow business. You ready for your bi-weekly trim?"

"Yep. I'd like you to make me look like Sean Connery this time."

"How about that. Last time you wanted me to make you look like Clark Gable. Hmmmm. Sean Connery. Sheriff, you just as well give up; you're never gonna look like any of those dudes you ask for; I'm a barber, not a plastic surgeon."

As the sheriff seated himself in the chair, the barber asked, "Have you heard about Elmer Bledsue?"

He answered, "No, what about Elmer?"

The barber continued, "Well, ya know, he decided to go on one of them cruises."

The sheriff answered, "Yes, I remember hearing talk that old Elmer was taking a cruise to somewhere, and I haven't seen him for a spell. Why, did he take the cruise?"

127

Carl Otto

"Well he took the cruise alright. And he came back home last night with a new bride."

"Oh, get outa here. Elmer came back with a bride? Why, that old confirmed bachelor is scared to death of women."

"Yeah, I know he was, but not any more. He sure came home with a woman; and she ain't a bad looker either; and she must be at least fifteen years younger than Elmer."

About that time, Ed Ashton came in saying, "Have you guys seen old Elmer Bledsue today. You're not gonna believe what I just saw."

The barber answered, "We were just talking about Elmer and his new bride."

Ed continued, "His new chick must be twenty years younger than he is, and she is a knockout."

The sheriff said, "Maybe he answered one of those adds in a magazine and has bought himself a Russian bride."

Then somebody said, "Yeah, he would have to buy a woman to get one like that. Good gravy, old Elmer is bald and fat and backward, heck, he don't have anything going for him."

Then one of the guys who had come in the barbershop and joined into the conversation said, "She ain't no Russian; or if she is, she shore speaks good southern American. I heard her talk."

Whatever Happened To Elmer

While they were discussing the news about Elmer, two more guys came in the shop telling they had just seen old Elmer down at the Café with his new bride.

The sheriff thought, "I guess the whole town is buzzing about this turn of events. Of course, it is news in any small community when a confirmed old bachelor, who is nearly sixty, suddenly gets married; especially when the bride is young enough to be his daughter. And, added to that, the bride is a 'looker' and Elmer is anything but a looker. Elmer is nearly bald, he is at least fifty pounds overweight, he had a ruddy complexion that shows evidence of at least a half dozen skin cancers, and to be right frank, he just ain't very good looking."

As the barber was putting the final touches on the sheriff's haircut, who would you guess appeared in the barbershop doorway? You guessed it; Elmer opened the door for his new wife and she stepped into the barbershop ahead of him.

Carl Otto

He said, "Gentlemen, I want you to meet my wife. This is Mrs. Elmer Bledsue, but she prefers to be called Dixie. Ain't she a dandy?"

Dixie smiled and said, "Hi y'all. It's mighty nice to meet y'all. If y'all are friends of Elmer, I'm sure y'all will be friends of mine too."

Everyone just stood with mouths wide open for a short moment before they all together responded, "It's nice to meet you Dixie."

Then she and Elmer continued on down the street.

That bunch of guys didn't wait long enough for them to be out of earshot before the speculation began.

One of them said, "You reckon she's a hooker?"

Another responded, "Why of course she's a hooker!"

The Sheriiff intervened, "Now, hold on a minute fellas. Don't be too quick to judge. She might be a real nice person. We all know Elmer; and I don't think there is a one of us who actually thinks he could be slickered by a woman."

"Oh, sheriff, be realistic, she has to be a hooker or a gold digger. No pretty young woman like that would take up with Elmer if she didn't have a reason."

A different guy speculated, "She must think old Elmer is rich."

Another said, "Huh! If she only knew, he don't have a pot to pee in."

Whatever Happened To Elmer

The sheriff added, "Hey, Fellers. He does own that farm. How many acres are in that place?"

One of the guys said, "My son farms the place next to him and he says Elmer has about three hundred acres out there; maybe more."

After a long thoughtful pause, the barber asked, "Have you guys ever seen Elmer wearin anything cept a pair of overalls."

Ed added, "Hey Guys, he doesn't only have that farm, I bet he has two cents out of ever nickel he ever made. Only the banker could tell you how much he has. Heck, he might not even know. Old Elmer could have his loot buried in fruit jars all over his farm."

One of the guys speculated. "Do you reckon he really is married to that girl? All we have is his word that she is his wife."

The barber answered, "Hey Charlie, you know better than that. They ain't another guy is this county whose word is any better than Elmer's; if he says he's married, then he's married."

Then the sheriff intervened, "You know something, Guys? If we are making all these speculations, here in the barbershop, what do you reckon is going on down at the beauty shop with the women folks? I think we better just back off a little and see what happens down the line a few months."

Carl Otto

The barber added, "I think the sheriff is right."

Sheriff Mayberry left that barbershop thinking, "Oh Lord, this is all I need. Some fancy talking little slicker moving into the community and taking some gullible old farmer for all he has. And, there is not a dad gummed thing I can do about it."

Then he said to himself, "You darn skeptic, that girl might mean well. And Elmer sure looks happier than I have ever seen him look, but this match simply don't make sense. But, I have to consider this from a positive point of view."

Three days later Deputy Frisbie tells the sheriff, "As I was coming to work, I saw Dixie and Elmer going into old Doc Osborne's clinic. You reckon he already has her in the family way?"

Then he just dropped into his chair and began laughing.

The sheriff added, "Or, maybe his Viagra prescription has run out."

They both started laughing like a couple of silly teenagers.

Then the deputy said, "Maybe he had her already in the family way and he had to marry her."

The sheriff added. "Or somebody else got her that way and she convinced Elmer he was the daddy."

Finally the sheriff said, "Hold on a minute Frisbie. Here we are; gossipin like a couple old biddies and snikerin like a

Whatever Happened To Elmer

couple or ornery teen-aged boys. We ought to be ashamed of ourselves."

"Well, we ain't doin nothing the whole town ain't doin."

It turned out they were both wrong. Dixie had convinced Elmer he should see a doctor about the skin lesions on his face. Doc's nurse later told her husband how happy Doc was that Dixie talked Elmer into coming to him. He did remove several pre-cancerous tumors from Elmer's face. He also gave Elmer a complete physical and suggested he lose some weight. Now Elmer is on a diet and is looking better with every passing week.

Elmer never confided in anyone as to where he met Dixie or where she was from. They all assumed he met her while on that cruise. The sheriff decided to do a little detective work.

He said to himself, "I am going to find out where Dixie came from."

The first thing he did was contact the cruise line on which Elmer was supposed to have booked his vacation.

He figured, being a law officer, he could find out from the cruise line office, the names of all the passengers who were on that particular trip. They were very cooperative. He found that Elmer had booked the cruise, but he requested a refund before the deadline arrived, so he never made the cruise; and they had no record of a passenger named Dixie. So the sheriff decided to ask Elmer the first time he had the

Carl Otto

chance. Only thing about that approach, every time Elmer came to town, Dixie came with him. They were like a pair of Siamese twins, and they seemed happier than a pair of chickadees.

Elmer continued to lose weight; he started wearing jeans and western shirts; he sported a new pair of cowboy boots and a new Stetson hat, and everyone was talking about how great "old Elmer" was looking now days; Dixie never changed a bit; she looked exactly the same as she did the first day in town.

Then one Sunday morning, they both showed up unannounced at the local Community Church. The congregation was buzzing. Even the preacher was flabbergasted to the point he got his notes mixed up and missquoted the Bible three times.

All through the sermon, whispers were heard:

"What ever happened to Elmer?"

"Why, I heard he married a hooker."

"My goodness, she is young enough to be his daughter."

"That young woman shore ain't no hooker."

Elmer and Dixie were appropriately dressed, and they looked as nice as any couple in attendance that morning.

Someone speculated, "My Lord, I'll bet old Elmer has lost thirty pounds."

During the time in the service where announcements were made, one of the ladies stood and announced, "I would like to have a short meeting with the members of the Ladies Aid Society in the meeting room before we go home for dinner."

It was obvious to all that this unscheduled meeting was for the purpose of discussing whether or not Dixie should be invited to be a member.

And, after the Bledsue's appeared in church four Sundays in succession, the speculations about them were beginning to change a bit.

One lady was overheard saying, "I don't think there is nearly as much difference in their ages as we thought."

Another said, "I think you're right. Elmer looks a lot younger since he has lost all that weight and started wearing something other than bib overalls. My Lord, what has happened to Elmer?"

Another congregation member said, "Who would have thought Elmer Bledsue could sing? And that Dixie has a beautiful voice. They stand directly behind us, so I can hear both of them very plainly."

The president of the Society did finally ask Dixie if she would like to join the organization.

She answered, "Oh my, Goodness. I have never been a person who joined ladies clubs, and I am certainly honored that Y'all have asked me to join. Do I need to give you an answer today?"

Carl Otto

"No. You talk it over with Elmer. You may let me know if and when you might want to join."

On their way home, Dixie said, "Did you hear what Mrs. Whettle asked me?"

Elmer answered, "Yes Dixie, I heard."

"What do you think I should do?"

"Dixie, I really hate to influence you in a decision like that, but I have always been honest with you so, - - - "

She interrupted, "So continue to be honest with me. Do you think I should join that club?"

"No Dixie, I do not think you should join. We live in the country and most of the ladies who belong to that club are town ladies. And, to be perfectly honest, Mrs. Whettle is nothing but a gossiping busybody."

"Now Elmer, y'all shouldn't talk like that. She was nace to me."

"You're right. I shouldn't talk like that. But I still don't think you should join that club unless you really would like to be a member."

"Honestly, I like those people at church, and I am enjoying getting to know people, and I want to help with their fund raisers and their special events; however, I have no desire to join the club."

"Then it's settled. You don't join. And, I will call Mrs. Whettle and tell her I would much rather you spend all your time with me."

Whatever Happened To Elmer

"Oh Elmer, you will do that for me?"

"Of course I'll do that for you. I will just be telling her the truth."

Three months had passed before the sheriff decided he was going to drop in on the Bledsues for a visit. Elmer's, place was located five miles west and three miles south of town near the river bottom. His house sat at the end of a long lane, behind a grove of trees, where it could not be seen from the road by passers by. The sheriff had been there several times so he expected to see the same old run-down house and out buildings that he remembered from his last visit.

Wow! Was he ever wrong; the house and every building had fresh coats of paint. The house had new dark green shingles; the yard was clear of all junk; there were flowers and shrubs all around. He just stood with his mouth gaping as Dixie came out on the front porch to welcome him.

She said, "Well, good morning Sheriff. What brings y'all the way out here?"

He then looked toward the barn where Elmer appeared in the doorway.

"Howdy Sheriff. Does the old place look a bit different?"

The sheriff said, "Elmer, I am completely bowled over. Did you two do all this repair, painting and clean-up work?"

Elmer answered, "Actually Sheriff, Dixie did the most of

137

Carl Otto

it. I told you the day I introduced you to her that she was a dandy. Now all this proves it doesn't it?"

The sheriff answered, "I am impressed!"

Then Elmer added, "Come on in and look at what she done on the inside."

He continued, "She's a painter, a paper hanger, a decorator. Heck Sheriff, they ain't nothing she can't do. Why she even got up on top the house and helped me put the new shingles on.

Dixie said, "Oh Elmer, quit yer braggin about me and Y'all sit down while I fix us a pitcher of lemonade."

Sheriff Mayberry looked around that old house, and it took him back forty years. All the furniture was antique, because that old house was still furnished with the same furniture Elmer's parents used; however, every piece had been stripped and restored. The house looked more like a well-kept museum than a living quarter. The sheriff was truly impressed.

Then he said, "Elmer, I have a confession to make. I was nosy enough that I went and meddled into something I had no business meddlin into."

Elmer interrupted him saying, "Heck, Sheriff, I knowed you would sooner or later. You found out I never did go on no cruise didn't ya?"

He answered, "Guess I didn't have you fooled, did I?"

138

Whatever Happened To Elmer

He continued, "I know it ain't any of my business. But just where did you come from Dixie."

Elmer spoke up, "It's a long story Sheriff, and it started during the Viet Nam War. You see, my platoon leader was Dixie's daddy; he was also like a pappy to me. When the war was over and we came back home, he went to his place in Mississippi and I came back here. We kept in touch all through the years, but we never had a chance to visit. Then a month or so before I went on that 'cruise.' I got a letter from Dixie saying her pappy was dying. So I decided I had to go see him."

He continued, "I don't know why I decided to stick to that story about going on a cruise; I guess I just didn't want anybody to know where I was or what I was doing. At first, I really was goin on the cruise, but when I got the letter from Dixie, telling me about her daddy, I changed my mind. Anyway, while I was down there, helping my old friend die, I got to know Dixie, and for some unexplainable reason, she took a fancy to me."

Dixie broke in at this point, saying, "It is more than just a fancy. You see, all my life I have heard my old daddy tell what a great guy this Elmer is. And then when I got married two different times to two different losers, I had just about convinced myself there were no good men in this world, except my old daddy. But when Elmer came down there to spend time with my daddy during his dying days, I saw how

Carl Otto

right my old daddy was about him. He is a kind, gentle, caring, loving man, and I fell in love with him, and I don't care if he is a few years older than me."

Right then Elmer added, "You would never know it by looking at her, but she is fifty-one years old."

She took a playful swat at Elmer saying, "Now, y'all didn't have to say that."

Then Elmer added, "I don't have to tell you why I fell for her. Heck, anybody with any sense at all would fall for her. I was just so surprised she fell for me."

He went on to say, "The thing that really knocked the wind out of me is when her daddy told me about how she had taken a fancy for me, and that he wanted the both of us to get married before he kicked the bucket."

Dixie added, "Elmer just couldn't believe I really wanted to marry him, at first, but I convinced him I was past ready to settle down with a good man. So, we fetched the local preacher, and my daddy gave me away from his deathbed."

When the sheriff left Elmer's place, he turned to both of them and said, "It is amazing how people's minds can just go wild speculating. I'll have to admit that I was as bad as any of them. When I get back to town, I am going to set some folks straight."

Elmer stopped him, saying, "No Sheriff, we don't want you to tell anyone of what you have found out here today. We both think we can serve as good examples to anyone

Whatever Happened To Elmer

who has a tendency to jump at conclusions. The truth of the matter is, I am a person who has always looked older than my actual years, and Dixie is a person who has always looked younger. The fact is, I am 57 and she is 51. She has inspired me to lose weight and start taking care of myself. We have started going to church, and we want everyone who has judged us, to eventually see us as who we are; just a happily married couple, enjoying our lives together, while living in an ordinary rural community. And we intend to do that by just being ordinary citizens."

THE END

IT REALLY IS YOU

IT REALLY IS YOU

A week or so ago, Eric Krueger picked up a copy of the local University Newspaper. Having been a graduate of that institution over fifty years ago, he remains interested in a few of the campus activities. As he glanced at the numerous coming events listed, he noticed there was a lecture scheduled in which a German author by the name of Ruskina Brenner, who was touring the United States, would be in one of the activity rooms at the Student Union Building where she would deliver a lecture which would be followed by a book signing of her latest work. Having nothing better to do, he decided to attend the event.

He went to the University on the date of the lecture, parked in the visitor parking lot and made his way across campus to the Student Union Building. The lecture was to be held on the second floor in what was called the "Green Room."

He entered the room and seated himself on one of the folding chairs on the back row. There were probably twenty students already seated and more were entering the room. To the right of the small podium was a folding table on which there were several stacks of books and to the left of the podium was an easel with a life-sized torso color picture of Ruskina Brenner. Assuming the picture was fairly current, it was obvious this visitor from Germany was an elderly individual; her beautiful wavy hair was snowy white; she was dressed in what appeared to be a gray business suit and she was wearing a lavender colored blouse with a ruffled collar. The picture was that of a very attractive elderly lady.

The lecture was scheduled to begin at 1:p.m. but it was nearly 1:30 before a petite, slightly stooped and a bit chubby old woman and a professor from the English department entered the room and made their way to the front of the room to the location of the podium. The professor made a short statement about a luncheon going overtime and then introduced Ms. Brenner.

The first thing she said, in her obvious German accent, was, "I hope you volks vill hexcuse me vor zittink on zis sthule, but you zee, I am no longer a youngster zuch as you students. Und I zeem to do my best tinking vile I am on my behint zetting, hokay."

This opening statement brought a wave of chuckles and a small round of applause from the audience, which had grown to the point where most of the chairs were filled. Eric looked around the room for another more mature face, but his and that of the lecturer appeared to be the only individuals in the room who were not students or young faculty members.

Ms. Brenner began her talk with a frank statement. "I zuppose already you have zeen zis stek uf books on zis table." She gestured toward the table and the books.

It Really Is You

"Vell, za main reason for mine beink here iss vor to zell my book, und I hope by za time I haf told you somzing about my life, you vill all rush up here und purchase von. Zat vay I can leave here today vit a big fet bag uf money. Hokay?"

Eric was thinking, "I like this old gal. Nothing starts a relationship, whether it be one-on-one or with a group of total strangers, better than pure frank honesty."

She continued with the usual statement about being honored to appear as a guest of the University, with accolades about the campus, the luncheon she had just attended, the friendliness of the students and faculty she had met thus far and ordinary statements made by nearly all speakers.

She then said, "My book iss about my life, as I vent from a small confused little girl who hat zuddenly lost all da members uf her family to a crewl Nazi dictatorship, to a middle aged voman who, hafing zurfifed two husbands, sree children und two step children, fount herself alone, confused und afraid again."

She continued, "Da vorld iss vell avare uf da autrocities zat vas committed on da Chews, but nussink much has effer been zaid about da autrocities vot vas on za Christians committed. How many uf you young volks are avare zat, in addition to za zix million Chews zat vere hexterminated, zere vere also tousants uf Christians eliminated by da Nazis?" "Among da tousants vas several huntret Catholic Priests."

147

Carl Otto

This was news to Eric. He was in Germany when WWII ended, so he was well aware of the concentration camps, but he was never told about Christians being killed in those death camps.

"I vill start by tellink you zat I vas a very heppy child right up to za day ven my whole vorld vell apart. I neffer new vy or vere my parents und brozzers und zizters vent. All I knew vas zat two big vemon came und took me avay von day und I nefer heard of any uv my vamily again. I zpent a goot part uf my adult life trying to vind out vere zey vent, but I vas nefer able to vind a traze uf zem."

"Unt, zen in za spring uf 1945 I hat a hexperienze vit an American zoldier who vas kint to me. Hiss ects uf kindness has been a drifing vorce vor me to come to America. I vas a zwelve yearz olt who vas liffing vit anozer group uf children in a home vor orphan chidren ven von day I vas standink by za side uf a bombed out building, by myzelf; unt I vas looking across da vay to an American zoldier who vas zitting on za front uf a cheep, eating a box lunch uf zome kind."

She continued, "Ve hat been tolt to ztay avay from zese zoldierz, und I hat been just zat doing, but zis zoldier looked to me like he vas not much more zan himself a kit, zo I did not hide, I just stood zere at zis young man looking."

"Zuddenly he looked up und zaw me. At virst I back arount za corner shrank, but zen I took anozer peek; he vas still at me looking. Zis time I stood zere beck to him looking."

148

It Really Is You

As Eric sat and listened to this lady tell her story, a memory began to surface in his mind; a memory of an event that took place in the spring of 1945, in a bombed out little town of Furth, Germany.

He thought, "Oh for crying out loud! This cannot be. It would be like one chance in a hundred million."

Eric stood up by his chair. He supposed most of the people assumed he was leaving, since he was sitting in an end chair on the back row. However, when he did not leave, Ms. Brenner looked in his direction and stopped talking.

She asked, "Do you haf for me a qvestion zir?"

Eric stood motionless for a moment as every eye in the room turned toward him and every mind was wondering what this old man had to say.

He took a deep breath and asked, "Did that young soldier motion for you to come to him?"

Hesitating a moment, she answered, "Yez he did."

Eric continued, "And, did that young soldier give you a small piece of chocolate candy?"

She was beginning to show a shocked look in her face, "Yez he did."

"And did he repeat this scene every day for quite a number of days?"

She placed her hands to the sides of her face.

Eric continued, "And did he call you Ruskie?"

"He called me Ruskie! Ach Mein Gott! You are no longer

149

zat young soldier, but I can zee zat you are za man who vas zat young zoldier. Iss it really you?"

"Yes, I was that young soldier."

Eric started moving toward the front as she came running to meet him with her arms extended. They met about half way.

Neither of them said a word; they just held each other; she was crying and he shed tears of joy along with her as a stunned audience looked on.

After several minutes Eric leaned back and held her face between his hands, "Ruskie, you little bugger, you're not a lot bigger than you were back there in Furth over sixty years ago."

"I tought you ver da handsomest man in da vorld, Und you hafent changed all zat much."

It Really Is You

She went back to the front of the room, pulling Eric along as she went. She retrieved her purse and dug out a small tattered black and white picture of a little girl and Eric, as a young soldier, standing in front of a sign that read RADFAHREN IM SCHULHOF VERBOTEN. (Bicycles in schoolyard forbidden)

"Anozer zoldier gif to me zis picture after you ver gone already, und in mine book iss a story about you, along vit enlarched copy from zis picture."

Eric looked at the picture and remembered the day they stood in front of that sign. In his meager collection of other

151

Carl Otto

pictures of long ago, he has another picture of himself and a buddy standing on that same spot. He also has a copy of the same picture she held in her hand.

In the happiness and the confusion of the moment, a voice was heard saying,

"Boy this is quite a set-up. Talk about a book selling promotion, this one tops them all."

Ms. Brenner heard the voice and immediately held up a hand quieting the crowd.

"I can zee ver zome uf you vold zink zis is fake, but to proof zis iss not, I am going to giff efervone in zis room one uf my books, free vor charge. I em zo heppy right now, I don't care about zelling books. In fect, za meeting iss ofer. I only vant to zee my long lost friend."

The two of them walked over to the side of the room where a sofa and some padded chairs were located. They seated themselves on one of the sofas.

Eric said, "As I recall, you were about nine years old when we had that picture taken. That would make you about seventy-one now because I am eighty."

"No, I vas almost tirteen year olt ven zat picture vas taken; I chust vasn't ferry big vor my edge. I em now zeventy-vife."

"Ruskie, I have thought about you so many times, and I remember those days when you would come to me and I would give you candy or some other food. I have always

It Really Is You

wondered whatever happened to you. Gosh, I didn't know you were only five, closer to four, years younger than me, or I might have tried to get romantic with you."

"It iss a goot zing you didn't know I vas olter; I vasn't very big, but I vas beginning to be a voman, und I vould haf been fery fulnerble vor you."

They laughed and they were joined in that laughter by a group of students who had come to talk to them.

One young lady said, "I think we have just witnessed the greatest love story ever."

Another remarked, "What are the chances of a reunion such as this ever happening; and what are the chances of it happening in front of so many witnesses?"

Eric answered questions and Ruskie answered questions and signed her book for a full hour before the English professor insisted they be left alone to enjoy their reunion.

As they left, Eric asked, "Where are you staying and how long will you be here?"

"I em in za Holiday Inn staying, und I em zupposed to be in Omaha from za day after tomorrow."

"Are you traveling by yourself or is someone with you?"

"I trafel vit myself, but my puplisher makes za arrangements vor book zignings und my blaces vor to stay. Und vere do you liff? Do you in zis town liff?"

153

Carl Otto

"Yes I live in one of those retirement villiages right here. I sold my home and moved there six years ago when my wife passed away."

"I vant to zee vere you liff."

"Hey kid, if you're waiting on me you're wasting your time; let's hit the road."

"Vait a minute. I not understand zat last vords."

Eric took her by the hand. "Come with me. My car is in the parking lot. We will go to my place and later we will go out for dinner. How does that sound?"

"Zat zounds vunderful. By za vay, I don't efen know your name. I remember za first name vas Eric, but I neffer knew your vamily name; vot it iss?"

"My family name is Krueger."

"Eric Krueger, acht tsu leiber, sie ist Deutch. Sprechen sie Deutch?"

"I did at one time know a lot of German, but if you don't use it, you lose it. I don't remember enough to carry on a conversation."

"Zat is okay, I haff learned to spek English. So ve talk in English."

The professor who had introduced Ms. Brenner was still at the podium looking at some papers. They walked to the podium where Ms. Brenner asked, "Are any of my books here still?"

154

The professor chuckled and answered, "They did not last long; however, I do believe everyone who wanted a copy was able to get one, thanks to your generosity."

"Za books are uf little conzern. Only za miracle uf my vinding zis man is important to me now."

Eric took Ruskie to his place where he showed pictures of his late wife and their four children and families, and of all his brothers and sisters and their families. He told her of his life as a building contractor. While he was telling of all his relatives, Ruskie was keeping a mental tally of the numbers.

After awhile, she asked, "Do you know how many peoples are in your vamily?'

"I guess I don't. I have never stopped to take inventory."

"Vell, you haf named zeventy zix names. My goodness, how great it vould be to haff family. You zee, I am all alone. I haf no family zat I know uf. My virst husband und my own sree children ver all killed in a tragic train accident. Zen I later married an olter man who had two grown children from whom he vas estranged. Ven he died zey did not efen to hiss funeral come. I haff no idea vere zey are now, und I do not care to vind out.

"Oh my gosh, you lost three children? And, you have lost two husbands? You most certainly have had a tragic life. I am amazed you have survived as well as you have."

"Vell, I guess a person has to learn to roll vit za pinches."

Carl Otto

Eric chuckled, "Yes, I guess you certainly learned to roll with the 'pinches.'"

They just sat and looked at one another for a long moment before Eric asked, "Where do you live? Do you own a home or do you rent?"

"Ven I am beck in Chermany, I am lifink in a little apartment in Frankfort, zat za owner upkeeps vor me until I come beck."

"How much of your time do you spend on tours such as this present one?"

"Oh, quvite a bit. I lif vereffer I am at za moment. I do not own much of anyzing zince my zecont husband died, hexzept my lep top computer. I haf been writink books zince I vas tirty vife yearz olt. Vor zome reason, peoples zeem to enjoy vat I write, zo I hef make a good liffing from my writing. Ven I traffel, vitch iss a lot uf za time, I do not bozzer to take a lot of closing viss me. I just buy new stuff and donate za dirty ones to charity. In America, J.C. Penney iss great. I buy anyzing I neet at Penny's or Val-Mart."

Eric could not keep his mind from returning to those days in Furth, Germany when he gave food to that little girl, so many years ago. He was looking thoughtfully at Ruskina and trying to see the little girl in her old face.

She asked, "Eric, vot do you zee in me now? Do you zink I am lookink a little bit different zan you remember?"

It Really Is You

"Of course you look different. But you still have the same look in your eyes. You know, I have thought about you so many times over the years. I saw many children during those war days, but you are the only one I ever had any real contact with. You made an indelible impression on me and I have always wondered what ever happened to you."

"Unt you nefer hexpected to zee me again, did you?"

"I never even gave that a thought, because I knew things like this just do not happen."

"Vell, it did happen, didn't it? Unt here ve are fece to fece. Now vat do ve doink?"

Eric took a deep breath before he said, "Ruskie, I have something to say that might sound a bit crazy, and it might put you to flight immediately, but I am compelled to say it anyway."

"Vot are you talking about?"

"You are alone; you are independent and you have no strings attached. Is that not right?"

"Yez, I am chust a little old fet lady who iss all by herzelf alone."

Eric could not keep from chuckling as he answered, "Well, I am just a littler old 'fet' man who is also all by himself alone. And since you have no strings attached and I have no strings attached, why don't you just give up this book selling tour and just stay here with me?"

157

Carl Otto

She hesitated for a long moment as she looked Eric straight in the eyes. "Vait a moment. Do I ziz lest stetment unterstent? You are esking me to stay here and liff vit you?"

"Exactly. I am asking you to stay here and live with me."

"Oh my goodness! I sink zings are heppining too fest. My mint iz in a virl."

Eric went on, "Just think about it. You are seventy-five years old; I am eighty years old. You are alone and I am alone. Do you want to spend the rest of your life alone when you have a chance to be with someone you love?"

"No, I don't vant to spent za rest uf mine life alone ven I hef a chence to zpent it vis someone I luf, unt I do luf you. You hef nefer been avay from my mind, but I hef zome commitments made."

"You mean like that book signing in Omaha?"

"Ya, zat iss one uf zem, and zere are uzzerz."

"What would you think about me just packing up and going with you?"

"You vould do zat for me?"

"No. I'll do it for both of us. And then when your tour is completed, we can come back home."

"But Eric, you do not know me vell enough for making a life long commitment."

"Life long? How many more years do we have? The way I see it, we have a chance to have a few years of happiness together."

158

It Really Is You

He hesitated a moment and then continued, "Ruskie, I had a good woman in my first and only wife; I had her for over fifty three years, But she is gone now and I am alone. I still have a loving family, but when I close that bedroom door at night, I am so alone.

I am past eighty years of age, but that does not mean I am past wanting female companionship nor am I past longing to have a warm body beside me while I sleep."

"Oh Eric, zere are lots of olt vemon running arount looking for a goot man to hop in za seck vit."

Eric really laughed at her remark as he continued, "Yes, I know full well there a lot of old women ready to 'hop in the sack,' but there has to be the right chemistry between two people in order to make a relationship work. And right now, at this very moment, I feel that chemistry. When I look into your eyes and hold you in my arms, I feel that chemistry, and so do you. Is that not so?"

"Oh yez, Eric, I veel zat chemistry. But zis iss zo fest my head iss virling arount."

Eric leaned back in his chair and sat silently for a long moment.

Finally he said, "I have an idea. Why don't you go ahead with your trip to Omaha and maybe even the rest of your planned trips. What the heck, you can use this miraculous meeting of ours as a means to really give a boost to your book sales. You can consider my proposal, while you are

159

Carl Otto

traveling around this vast country, all alone. Then, while you are sleeping in those hotel rooms, all alone, you can seriously consider how great it would be to live the rest of your life with me."

"Zat iss a hexellent idea. I vill continue on my tour, unt I vill keep in touch."

Three weeks later.

Eric is awakened by the sound of his telephone ringing. He answered the phone on the fourth ring.

"Hello."

"Eric, zis iss Ruskina."

He threw back the covers and sat up on the edge of the bed.

"Ruskie! I had about given up on you. Where are you?"

"I am in Zeattle, unt zis iss za lest day from mine tour. I hef been a lot uf time spending on sinking about vot you zaid."

"And?"

"Do you still za same vey veel?"

"Of course I do."

"Zen you still vant me vor to come liff vit you?"

"Yes, without question."

"Eric, I am not a deeply relichious person, but I vill not liff vit a man who is not mine husband."

"Great! How soon can you get here? We will drive down to Miami, Oklahoma and get married."

160

It Really Is You

"Miami, Oklahoma? Vy zis place?"

"Because there is no waiting period. When can you be here?"

"I am zuposset to arrife into Kansas City day after from tomorrow, at sree p.m."

"Super! I'll be waiting at the airport."

"One more sing, Eric."

"What is it?"

"I neet to make a trip to Chermany to dispose of zome stuff und pick up zome stuff."

"No problem. I have always wanted to make a trip back there; we will go together, as man and wife. It can be our honeymoon trip, what do you think of that?"

"Oh zat is great. Unt vile ve are zere, ve vill go to Furth and haff our picture taken in zat zame school yard vere ve stoot zo many years ago."

"If that school is still there, we will certainly do just that."

"I can't vait to be wiss you and to meet all your peoples."

"I know they will love you."

"I vonce read an American poem zat zaid, 'I em trinkink vrom mine zauzer, cauze mine cup iss offervlowet."

"I know the poem. Yes, our cup has indeed over-flowed."

THE END

KID POWER

KID POWER

One year ago last Tuesday, Ed and Erma Heplar discussed divorce after eighteen years of marriage. The unusual and significant reason these two individuals sat down and actually discussed the subject came about when their two oldest children, fourteen year old Sam and his sister, thirteen year old Sara, announced one morning at the breakfast table they, had 'had it."

Sam said, "Mom and Dad, Sara and I have been worrying about you two long enough. We are sad that you don't love each other any more and we are tired of living with two people who hardly ever even talk to each other."

Erma started to say something but was cut off by her daughter, "Just don't talk Mom!" she yelled. "Sam and I are sick and tired of living in a house with parents who are so unhappy with each other. Just keep still and listen to Sammy."

Carl Otto

Erma was shocked and Ed was stunned by what their kids were saying, but both of them could immediately see the kids were deadly serious, so neither of them said a word as Sam continued.

"Us kids know that you both still love all of us, but we ain't dummies. We can all see that you two are not happy with each other. So we have decided we want you to get divorced."

Erma asked, "Have you talked this over with Tommy and Kelli?"

"Yes Mom, we have. Well, we didn't with Kelli, 'cause she's too young to understand, but we three oldest all decided last night that since I'm the oldest, I would tell you guys."

Ed was so stunned by this revelation that he just sat there like he had turned to stone as Sam continued.

"We know that lots of people get divorced anymore. Some of our friends parents are divorced and most of them tell us they don't like it, but it is better than living in a war zone."

Sara added, with a sarcastic tone in her voice, "I don't think I'm ever going to like get married. People just get all like gushie with each other; they hug and they kiss and they tell each other like 'Oh I just can't live without you!' Then they like get married and have kids and start getting fat and old; then all at once they like look at each other and say, 'Yuk! I don't even like this person anymore." She gestured

Kid Power

with her hands up even with her shoulders and turned outward. "Oh well we got kids, so we have to like make the best of it.' Fooey!!! Never me!" She left the room crying.

Sam continued, "I know neither one of you is having an affair with somebody; I guess you have both got too old for sex. I think that must have been all you ever liked about each other in the first place."

He went on, "Now we got it all figured out what you should do. First of all, we don't want no custody battles over us kids, because it ain't us that is tired of either one of you, so we all want to see both of you and be with you without any restrictions. In the second place, since dad is a farmer and he has a big workshop and we live on a farm, we think Mom and us kids should get the house; we can fix you (pointing toward his dad) a room out in the shop. You spend most of you time out there anyway. And, I might even stay out there some too."

Sam stood up from his chair. "There is just one other thing. We figure you must have liked each other quite a bit at first, so we want to know what happened. We want both of you to write down a list of things you liked about each other when you got married, and another list of things you don't like about each other now. Then Sara and I will read over the lists. We want to make sure it ain't our fault."

He turned to leave the room. "Here comes the school bus, we'll see you when we get home."

167

Carl Otto

There was dead silence for a full two minutes before Ed said, "Wow! What do you think of that?"

"I think our kids are smarter and more observant then we have given them credit."

"Erma, Sam is right. There was time when we did care. Maybe it is time we did take a close look at our alternatives."

"You are right, Sam IS right. So before another word is said, I too think we should take a good look at our situation. I will make the lists Sam and Sara have requested, if you will also make the lists. And then, I think we should show each other what we have written before we give the lists to the kids"

"Agreed. Maybe we can both learn something from this. I'll have mine here in the morning."

Ed got up from the table and left the house. He went out to his pickup, got in and headed for the pasture to check the cattle. He reached for the notebook in the glove box, on which he scribbled notes about the cattle or other things that needed attention.

He thought, "I'll write my lists in that notebook."

As he opened the notebook, the family picture he had scotch taped to the inside of the front cover seemed to jump right at him. He looked at the picture for a long moment.

He thought, "This picture was taken when Kelli was one year old. There I sit, with little Kelli on my lap and my arm around Tommy. Erma is standing behind me. She has

Kid Power

her left arm around Sam and her right arm around Sara. Good heavens, we are a happy looking family. Look at me. I think I must have gained thirty pounds since that picture was taken."

He sat in the truck a full five minutes before he got out to open the pasture gate. He then drove through the gate, got back out of the truck and closed the gate. As he returned to the truck and headed toward the cattle he looked at the picture again.

His mind recalled the day that picture was taken. "Erma had a coupon we had received in the mail that indicated this photographer would be at the Coop for a period of time, and as a promotion, would be taking family pictures of Coop members. She talked me into getting all dressed up in a suit and tie for the pictures. I protested, and we argued, but she prevailed. This is a copy of the only good family picture we have. There is a twelve by fourteen inch copy on the wall in the front room."

Another memory occurred as he thought about the picture. "The night we had that picture taken, Erma and I had one heck of a fight. She wanted me to get a vasectomy and I blew my stack. I said, 'Oh no, not me. I am not going have my manhood carved on."

He mumbled aloud to himself, "She told me, four children were enough, and that she afraid of the pill because there is a history of cancer in her family."

169

Carl Otto

He continued to recall the incident. "Because of my bull-headedness, she did continue taking the pill. Three years later she had to have a hysterectomy, and she did have a cancer. Luckily it was completely contained, but from that day on she has never been the same. It has now been nearly a year since we have slept together."

Ed stopped the truck and leaned his head down on his folded arms across the steering wheel. He said aloud, "My God! What a meathead I have been."

He suddenly was overcome with an emotion he had never experienced. Tears were streaming from his eyes and he was having difficulty breathing as his big frame shook with every sob.

When he did regain his composure he continued talking to himself, "Oh Lord, I am thirty eight years old and I have been bawling like a baby. I guess if I am half the man I claim to be, I will go back to the house and tell Erma exactly what has just happened to me. To heck with the cattle."

He turned the pickup around and headed for the house.

Arriving back to the house, he got out of his truck and headed straight for the kitchen door. As he entered he saw Erma sitting at the table making the lists Sam had requested. She looked up at Ed, and she could readily see he was upset, but she said nothing.

Ed sat down in a chair across from Erma. He sat silently for a moment before he finally spoke.

Kid Power

"Erma, I have come to the conclusion that I am a real stupid meathead."

She never answered or changed the expression on her face. She continued to look down at her paper.

He went on to tell her about how he had been looking at the family picture; about how he remembered the way he had protested and didn't want the picture; about the fight they had over the vasectomy and her reluctance to take the pill and about how selfish and foolish he was concerning her fear of the pill.

He held back his emotions as best he could as he added, "That cancer could have killed you."

She looked up from her writing and said, "I still have eight more years to sweat out before I know for certain it was totally contained."

Erma never changed her somber expression. She sat with a pen in her hand and a paper on the table in front of her. It was like she did not even hear what Ed had just said to her.

Finally she said, "I have been sitting here trying to think of the reasons I ever took up with you in the first place. Since I was a country girl, I thought it was great that you were so active in FFA. I was impressed because you were a great football player and I thought it was great when the other girls reminded me my boyfriend was usually high point man in the basketball games, and that you set a new school record with the shot-put. You never were very handsome,

Carl Otto

but somehow girls were attracted to you and since you were attracted to me, I thought I was the bell of the ball. What did you see in me?"

Ed sat for a moment before he answered, "Well, I guess I saw what all guys are looking for. A sexy, pretty girl who thinks a guy is cool. But there was more than that. I liked the way you always smelled so clean and that you never wore a lot of make-up. I was always impressed with how great you looked in those freshly washed, starched and ironed dresses. I liked your hair and your eyes and I loved to hear you laugh. And I remember another thing that impressed me. I never heard you badmouth any of the other girls, and they all seemed to like you."

She had an almost shocked look as she answered, "We have been married eighteen years, Ed, and this is the first time I have ever heard you say any of those things. Now I am wondering if you ever actually felt that way. I've heard your friends tell about how good you are at telling stories and b.s.'ing people."

"I don't know what to say Erma. I know neither one of us is the same person we were eighteen years ago; heck, between the two of us we have gained a good fifty pounds."

"Fifty pounds!" She laughed, "I think you have gained that much. If I remember, you weighed 190 when we married and I'll bet you weigh at least 240 now. I weighed 115 when we married; my last doctor's visit I weighed in at

172

152. So we're both porkies and we both know we need to lose weight."

"Yes, and I know what you're going to say next. You're going to tell me how you can't stand that 'little pinch of snuff.'"

"I didn't say it; you did. I never could understand why anyone would take up that filthy habit."

"I guess this is a good illustration of how much attention you have paid to me lately."

"What do you mean by that?"

"I mean I have not put a dip of smokeless tobacco in my mouth for nearly three months. I have not mentioned it because I was not convinced I could quit it completely. Now I think I have it whipped. The only problem has been, I think I have gained a few pounds."

"Ed, I am impressed. Now, have you noticed anything different about me?"

"Yes. Your hair is shorter and you are letting the gray hair stay."

"Well, you did notice. But you never let me know you noticed. You remember I told you I weighed 152 when I last visited my doctor. Well, I now weigh 143 pounds, and my goal is 125."

A concerned look came over Ed's face. "Is there a reason why you had to lose weight after you went to the doctor?"

"Only that I needed to lose weight. He put me on a restricted fat and lower calorie diet, and it is working."

Carl Otto

"Maybe I should go see him and have him put me on a diet."

Erma reached over to the counter and picked up the telephone; she handed it to Ed and said, "555 – 5000."

"That's his number?"

"That's his number."

Ed dialed the number. After a pause, "I would like to make an appointment for a complete physical." — — — "Next Wednesday at 10:30 AM. I'll be there."

Ed hung up the phone and then sat for a moment before he said, "Erma, I don't want to break up our marriage."

"Don't you think it is already pretty well cracked?"

"Maybe it's time we get out the duct tape."

He stood up and started to leave. Erma called after him.

"What are you going to do about this list Sam and Sara have asked us to compile?"

He stopped and turned toward her. "The question is, are you ready to give our marriage another chance?"

"I think we should tell the kids we are having difficulty, but we are working on a solution. Maybe we should ask for an extension of the deadline."

"Good idea."

Ed went back out to his truck and headed back to the pasture. Sara stood at the door and watched the pickup go through the barnyard gate before she sat back down at the table.

Kid Power

She thought, "I think Ed actually has been crying. His eyes looked a bit red and his lip made a few slight quivers when he mentioned that cancer could have killed me."

She mumbled aloud to herself, "How can two people date each other for three years, be married for eighteen years, have four children and engage in a family business, be intimate and passionate with each other for the better part of those years, and still not really know each other?"

"Have I ever looked Ed straight in the eye and said, "I love you Ed."

She thought, "I don't think I have ever told Ed I loved him, and I cannot recall his ever using those words with me. Neither of us had parents who were very demonstrative. I guess neither of us was ever conditioned to use the word. I know I never heard my dad tell anyone he loved them. I guess it was always just assumed. Assumptions don't cut it."

When Ed came to the house for lunch, he discovered Erma dressed in a pair of jeans and a loose fitting Sweatshirt and sneakers. She had her hair tied up behind her head with a ribbon.

"I didn't fix lunch. Let's go to town and have a sandwich."

Ed looked a bit surprised, but he did not hesitate to go along with the idea. "Just a second, while I go wash up."

He went to the bathroom and began washing his hands. As he washed he thought, "I have not seen her in a pair of jeans for I don't know when. I guess she wants to let

175

Carl Otto

me see for sure how much weight she has lost. Actually, she looks great."

Going back to the kitchen, Ed discovered Erma was already waiting in the pickup, so he hurried out. As he got into under the wheel, he said, "It's been awhile since I have seen you in jeans. You look great. I can sure see you have lost weight."

"According to the bathroom scales, I have lost nineteen pounds."

"Wow. Now, as I really pay attention, I can see it in your face too."

"Today I am breaking over. I want a big juicy hamburger with onions, lettuce, pickles, tomatoes and the works; and I want fries and a Pepsi."

"I guess I'll have the same thing, but I'm afraid I won't be breaking over any. Unless it makes my belly break over my belt a little more."

Erma chuckled at that remark

When the kids got home from school, Sam went straight to the kitchen where his mother was usually preparing dinner; however, today she was not preparing a meal.

He said, "Where is dad, and where are the lists?"

"Your dad is taking a shower. He will be in here before long and then we are going to have a family meeting. Tell Sara and Kelli and Tommy we want them here too. All of you go ahead to your rooms and do your homework, if you have any, I will call you later."

Sara appeared in the kitchen door. "Mom! You are wearing jeans and a Sweatshirt. And you have your hair tied back. What's the deal?

"We are going to have a family meeting, and then we are all going to town for dinner at the Chicken House."

"You mean all of us together, at the same time?"

"Do think we can handle that?"

Sara dropped her backpack on the floor, ran to her mom and threw her arms around her. "Oh Momma, you mean we're going start being a real family?"

"I don't know exactly what it all means Honey." She held out her left arm to Sam and he joined the three-way hug. "What I do know, is that you two have made your dad and me do some real hard thinking today."

"Did you make the lists?"

"We worked on them Sam, but we want an extension on the time limit, if you don't mind. But I can tell you without hesitation, the problems between your dad and me have nothing to do with any of you kids."

Ed's voice came from the doorway. "No kids, none of this is your fault. I am afraid the better part of our marriage problems have been mine. Let's all go into the front room and talk; you can take care of your homework later."

Carl Otto

They all went to the front room and seated themselves. Sam and Sara sat on the divan, Ed sat on his recliner and Kelli climbed onto his lap, Erma sat in her recliner and Tommy seated himself on the arm of her chair.

Ed started the meeting by saying, "This has been the first day in my life, and I'm thirty-eight years old, that I have been concentrating my thoughts on something other than my own little world. I have reviewed some things I have done in the past, and I am not very proud of myself."

Erma added, "It is not all your father's fault. I have made mistakes too."

"Okay, we have both made mistakes. But today your mother and I have had some good discussions. And we have not had a fight. We went to town together at noon today to have a hamburger. We pointed out some good things and some bad things about each other and we decided to try change. We don't want to break up our family."

Erma said, "We are not going to promise anything, because so many times promises end up being broken promises, but we are going to try to do better."

Ed then said, "Okay, Sam. Go out to the shed and get Grandpa's old Chevy out. Oh, I know you have been starting it regularly, and even taking it for a short drive once in awhile. So do you think you could chauffer the family to the Chicken House."

Kid Power

Sam had a sly grin as he answered, "I guess I didn't put much past you, did I?"

"The feeling is mutual. Your Mom and I haven't put much past you and Sara either, have we?"

Sam went out to bring the old green 1952 Chevrolet four-door sedan. When he drove it up to the side gate by the house Erma remarked, "Good gracious. I was aware Sammy loved that old car, but I sure never realized how much. He has it polished and shining like a new one."

They all got in and Sammy headed for town, with his dad and little Kelli in the front seat and his mom, Sara and Tommy in the back seat.

As they all got out of the car and headed into the Chicken House, Little Kelli stopped all of them and remarked, "Daddy, why are we all going to this place at the same time?"

Ed squatted down in front of her, pulled her close, and whispered into hear ear, "Honey, it's because your daddy didn't know how to take his family out for dinner, until Sammy and Sara taught me an important lesson."

She pulled her little head back and said loud enough for all to hear. "Sam and Sara taught you an important lesson?"

Ed stood up, reached out with his big arms and gathered Sam and Sara in an embrace. He never said a word because he was fighting back the tears.

Carl Otto

Erma could see Ed was about to lose his composure, so she spoke up, "Come on kids, let's get in there and get seated before Daddy decides to take us to the Greasy Spoon."

"Entering the Chicken House, they were greeted by a young woman who asked, "Smoking or Non Smoking?"

Sara quickly answered the question, "None of us are smokers."

Okay. Follow me."

She led them into what was obviously the family dining area. All, except three, of the tables were large enough to seat six or eight people and two of them were even larger.

Stopping at one of the medium sized tables, she asked, "How is this?"

Erma answered, "This will be fine."

"Your waitress will be here in just a moment."

As they were seating themselves, voices come from a nearby table. One said, "Hi Sam."

And another said, "Sara! Good to see you. How you doing?"

"Oh, Hi Dean, I didn't see you when I came in."

"That's cause it's a little dark in here and your eyes have got to get adjusted."

Erma turned toward the parents of the other kids and said, "I guess we haven't met you folks. We are Sam and Sara's parents, Ed and Erma; and this is Kelli and Tommy.

180

Kid Power

"We are Dean, Shelly, and Freddie's parents, Joe and Ilene Buck." The man said as he extended his right hand to Ed.

They all exchanged handshakes.

"Hey Sam, I ain't seen you guys here before. Do you come here very much? We eat here lots of times."

"Well, we eat their chicken, but most of the time we get carry out."

Ed spoke up, "But I think that is going to change. We do love their chicken, and I could eat a barrel of their slaw."

He hesitated a bit and added, "But I guess you can see I eat barrels of almost anything."

The waitress walked up with the menus. "May I have your drink orders while you look at the menus?

They all had chicken dinners and they enjoyed meeting and visiting with the family at the adjoining table. Sam and Dean were both ninth graders; Sara and Shelly were seventh graders, so the fact that the kids were classmates, made conversation easier.

In the back of Erma's mind, as they were headed home, was a feeling of distrust she could not shake. She kept thinking, "Oh well, at least we had a pleasant dinner that I didn't have to fix. - - - - and I think he had been crying. Oh, he never cries. - - - but, then he did get choked up when we were coming in. I wonder if he has really stopped using that snuff, Things have not been good, but at least they have been predictable. I just do not understand how Ed could be seri-

Carl Otto

ous about making such an about face, I think he is b.s.'ing me – and the kids. I wonder if I made a mistake by putting on these jeans and trying to look a little better. - - - He did seem sincere when he told me I looked great. - - But then again, he could be feeding me a line of bull."

Driving home from the Chicken House, Ed was thinking. "This was great today. -- - Erma looked nice in those jeans - - - well, she is still a bit of a chunk, but nothing like me - - but she looked nice. And the kids sure enjoyed the outing - - - those folks in the next table were nice - - but she is not saying much - - - I don't think she trusts me - - -huh, why should she? I really have been a turkey.   Why didn't I get one of those vasectomy jobs when she wanted me to?. — Oh boy! I don't think want a divorce - - - -in fact I'm sure I don't. But at the same time, I'm still in my thirties, and my wife refuses to sleep with me- - - that's going to have to change.- - -I came close to taking that gal at the stockyards on a date- - - Oh gadfry, I'm glad I didn't — -But I can't let my life be the main consideration. The kids come first. I have got to start working on getting things back to normal. I think, when I go to Doc for that physical, I'm going to tell him I want a vasectomy."

Ed's visit to the doctor's office revealed he is sugar intolerant. Which means he will most likely develop diabetes as he gets older. However, he is lucky the condition has been discovered early, because with a proper diet and a loss of

Kid Power

fifty pounds, he most likely will be able to go another ten years or so before he even has to take medication for the condition. It is probably predictable that he will eventually become diabetic, and will need to take insulin shots.

So, the doctor informed Ed he should start following the same diet he has prescribed for Erma. Ed agreed he would do the best he could to change.

Before Ed left the office he made an appointment for some out patient surgery at the local hospital. He did not want to give himself a chance to back out, so the appointment was for 6:am the very next morning. And, he did not want Erma to know about it until he was ready to tell her himself.

The next morning, around 10:30 am, Erma looked out in the driveway where she observed Ed getting slowly out of his pickup. She watched him as he walked, taking very short steps, toward his shop building.

She thought, "I'll bet he has wrenched his back again."

She continued to watch him as he entered the shop. "I better take him a couple of Tylenol tablets. I know he won't come to the house for them."

She went to the medicine cabinet and got the Tylenol. Then she drew a glass of water and headed out the door toward the shop.

When she entered the shop, she observed Ed sitting in an old beat up recliner he had out there.

Carl Otto

"Here, take these Tylenol. What did you do to your back?"

"It's not my back."

"Well, whatever it is, it is obvious you are in pain. Here take these."

"I can't take them because I am already on a pain medication."

She became concerned. "Why are you on a pain medication? What is the matter with you?"

"Well, damn it all, I am hurting because I have just come from the hospital where I had an operation."

"AN OPERATION!! What kind of an operation?"

"I have had that vasectomy you wanted me to get years ago. There I've said it. Now you know. "

"You had a vasectomy? You had a vasectomy!"

She started to chuckle.

"What is so funny about that?"

Ed, don't you remember? I have had a hysterectomy. I had it when they removed that cancer."

He got a shocked look on his face. Then he just slapped his big hands up to the sides of his head. "Oh Grrrr! What a dummy!"

Erma really started laughing. She could not contain herself.

"I'm sorry Ed, but this is funny. This is real funny."

Kid Power

She turned and leaned on the work bench as she went into convulsions of laughter."

"Why in the world didn't Doc remind me about that?"

Through uncontrollable chuckles, she continued, "Ed. Don't you remember? Doctor Bristow is retired. We have had a new doctor for years."

Then Ed started laughing. Between guffaws, he said, "We are not going to tell anyone about this."

"I don't know if I can keep this a secret or not"

"Oh yes you will! Oh, it hurts when I laugh."

"Oh I wish I could have had this scene video taped; we could have won $10,000 for the funniest home video."

Erma went to Ed and put her arms around him. "You big lug, you still thought enough of me to get a vasectomy, even when it was unnecessary."

"Yes Erma, I love you, and I will do anything to save our marriage. I would even let you sit on my lap right now."

"You have just saved our marriage. I don't ever want to sleep another night without you next to me. But, I don't think I had better sit on your lap for a few days."

Ed said, "The kids will be glad to hear this. But we will NOT tell the kids about this dumb stunt I have pulled. I am walking funny because I wrenched my back again. Right?"

The two of them headed for the house, with Erma's left arm around Ed's waist, Ed's right arm draped around

Erma's shoulders, Ed taking short slow steps and both of them laughing.

And, it all started with a nudge from their kids. Kid power.

The End

CONGO
AND
SAMANTHA

CONGO AND SAMANTHA

Jerry Couch graduated from Hard Rock Teachers College in the spring of 1949 along with an untold number of WWII veterans who had taken advantage of the G. I. Bill of Rights; a U.S. Government program that paid educational expenses of returning service men and women. It was a great program for so many returning veterans because it is fairly certain that a sizeable percentage of them would never have gone to college otherwise.

Jerry had a contract in his pocket with the Alfalfa, Oklahoma Public School System. In only a few more days he would be starting his career as an educator. His assignment is to coach all sports, teach health and physical education and be an instructor in a minimum of three undesignated classes at Alfalfa High School. The annual salary, as indicated in bold figures on the nine-month contract, called for a whopping $2800.00, to be paid in twelve equal payments of $233.34. Jerry had never made that kind of money in his life.

As he rolled down the highway in his 1931 Chevrolet Sedan, he was beginning to get more and more anxious for his new career to start. He was also anxious to see the town of Alfalfa and the building in which he would be working. He had seen neither, since the Principal of the school hired him during one of the Career Days at the college. He was

Carl Otto

aware the school was small, but Mr. Hodges had assured him the kids were "great kids" and the athletic program had a history of being competitive in their league.

Teachers were supposed to report to school on Tuesday morning, the day after Labor Day, for a day of orientation and introductions; the first day for students was scheduled for Wednesday. Mr. Hodges had already made arrangements for Jerry's housing. It seemed there was a "sweet little old lady" who operated a Boarding House for single teachers at "very reasonable" rates. Jerry was not choosy in that department.

When Jerry approached the city limits sign, it looked as if Alfalfa was very much like so many small towns in those days. He counted the businesses as he drove slowly down Main Street upon his arrival that Sunday afternoon. The thought was going through his mind, "This looks like a nice little town. I think I am going to like it here."

Finding the school building was no problem; it was located the second block south of the final building of the two blocks of businesses lining both sides of the street. An old Phillips 66 Service station was located directly across the street from the school. Jerry pulled in to fill up his gasoline tank.

An elderly man came out as he rolled to a stop beside the two antique hand-operated gasoline pumps. A sign in front of the building read, Regular 20 and Ethyl 22; Oil 35 cents per quart. Cold pop 10 cents.

"What'll ya have, Sonny?"

"Fill it up with regular, and you might check the oil. And, just how cold is that pop?"

"Ya better not have any bad teeth if ya take a swig of my pop."

Jerry went inside and walked to the pop cooler. When he lifted the lid and removed a bottle of Nu-Grape he discovered the old fellow was not kidding; the pop was almost frozen.

When the old fellow came inside Jerry extended his hand, "I'm Jerry Couch, the new coach at the high school."

"Well, it's good ta meet ya Jerry. I'm Wilbur Wright, but I'm not the one that built that plane. Hope you're a better coach that that lunkhead that's been here."

"Oh? I heard he was a good coach; that he just got a better paying job."

"Huh, That guy couldn't pour his own water out of a boot if the instructions were written on the heel. Oh, he had pretty fair teams, but that was because the kids were just good athletes."

"Well, I can't make any promises, but I intend to do my best."

Carl Otto

Jerry paid for the gasoline and pop and headed for his car. Suddenly he remembered he needed to find out where the boarding house was located. "Say, Mr. Wright."

"I'm not Mr. Wright, I'm just plain Wilbur."

"Okay, Wilbur it is. Could you tell me where I might find the little old lady, here in town, who rents rooms to teachers?"

"That would be Julia Monroe. Just turn around and head back down main like ya came to town. When ya get three blocks north of the Hardware store, grab a right. You will see her sign at the next corner."

Jerry thanked him, got in his old Chevy and headed for Mrs. Monroe's. The place was not hard to find; there was an artistically designed and skillfully painted sign in front of this huge old house. He pulled up to the curb and stopped. The old place looked more like one of those small town funeral homes. It appeared to have been freshly painted; the lawn was like a golf course green; the shrubs and flower arranged as if professionals had placed them. The thought crossed Jerry's mind, as he walked up the front steps, "I don't know whether or not I can get used to living in a fancy place like this."

A small sign on the front screen door was a friendly greeting. "Y-All come on in and stay a spell."

He opened the door and entered a foyer. The inside of the house was as impressive as the outside. The first thing

192

Congo and Samantha

he noticed was the open stairway. As he looked up the stairs his eyes continued on upward to a beautiful cut glass chandelier hanging a good fifteen feet above his head. While he was staring as the ornate fixtures, a voice greeted him.

"You must be our new Coach, Jerry Couch."

He looked down to see a very pretty little lady with snow-white hair and a million dollar smile.

"Yes, I am Jerry Couch. And I assume you are Mrs. Monroe."

"Everybody calls me Julie, or Granny. Are you ready to move into your apartment?"

"Oh, it is an apartment? I was expecting just a room."

"Heavens no. We couldn't treat our new coach like that. I have a nice two roomed apartment, with private bath for you."

"I'm not sure I can afford accommodations like that."

"The rent is fifty dollars each month."

"Do you serve meals?"

"I used to do that, but not any more; however, we do have an excellent café in town where meals are good and the prices are very reasonable."

"Sounds like a pretty good arrangement, Mrs. Monroe."

As she started up the stairs, she said, "And you have forgotten already; I am called Julie or Granny. And, by he way, there is a young widow woman here in town who will do your laundry if you are interested."

193

Carl Otto

"Yes, I am interested. How do I contact her?"

"You won't need to contact her; I'll do that for you. She comes here twice a week to pick up the laundry for all her customers, and I'll tell you Jerry, that girl can starch and iron a shirt as good as any Chinaman you ever heard of."

"Will I need to get some laundry bags?"

"Nope. I have a whole batch of old pillowslips; I'll put your name on a couple of them and we'll use them for laundry bags."

"How about getting my shoes shined and my hair cut, is there a service for that?"

She stopped walking, turned and looked up at Jerry over the top of her glasses.

He chuckled and said, "Granny, I was kidding about the shoeshine; I think I can handle that, but is there a barber here in town?"

"Yes, we have a good barber. Mort Milhouse has a shop right next to his house out in east town. He is open any time he is not fishing and he is fishing anytime the fishing is good, but he'll give you a haircut any time, at any hour, if he's home, for seventy-five cents."

"Sounds like a guy would have to call for an appointment."

"No, you can go out there most any time. If he's not there, his wife can give you a better haircut that Mort can. She isn't an official barber, and she don't charge for her haircuts, but

Congo and Samantha

it seems to be a gentleman's agreement when she cuts hair that a fellow drops a "tip" in the fruit jar by the door. And most of the time, the tip is a dollar."

Jerry grinned and answered, "Hmm, no wonder old "Mort" is such a fisherman."

The apartment was located at the end of a long hall upstairs. A neatly printed sign in the hallway spelled out the house rules. NO USE OF TOBACCO, NO USE OF ALCHOHOL NO LOUD MUSIC NO PETS. Jerry was well pleased with the entire arrangement. He moved all his stuff to his apartment, and then drove to the local restaurant to try the food. He was hungry.

While at the restaurant, he met so many friendly people there was no way he could remember all the names. He did remember one of the men told him the only problem he would have, as the new coach, would be with a big bully of a kid they called "Congo."

Jerry thought, "I can't wait to meet this so called problem. I am not a big man, but I am in excellent physical condition. I survived nearly three months of combat with the 82nd Airborne Div. During WWII, so I can say with confidence that no high school kid will intimidate me."

Tuesday morning arrived finding Jerry already at the school building before any of the other staff members, other than the head custodian, were present. The first day orientation included all employees from the cook's helpers right

195

Carl Otto

on down to the superintendent. Alfalfa school district em-ployees were in the auditorium before 8 a.m. The staff in-cluded: Two cooks, two custodians, three bus drivers, four elementary teachers, five high school teachers, one secre-tary and one administrator. The administrator, Mr. Hodges, also taught three high school classes. The total school en-rollment in grades 1 through 12 was 139 students. It was a typical plains state rural school.

Kids began showing up the next morning around 7:30 a.m. and by 7:45 the three buses were in and unloaded. All elementary and the high school kids came to the auditori-um. The superintendent/principal greeted the students and then introduced the staff members. He made a short pep talk to the entire group before dismissing the elementary students and their teachers and the support staff members.

After all the younger kids and their teachers had gone to their respective rooms, Mr. Hodges asked the five high school instructors to join him at the front of the room. This time he mentioned the fact that they had four new faculty members and he enumerated the classes each would teach. While he was talking there was a slight disturbance coming from a group of boys. He stopped his talking, slowly walked over in front of the boys in question and just stood there staring at them.

Jerry could see what the man at the restaurant was talk-ing about. He could also easily identify Congo. All of the

Congo and Samantha

boys settled down and even began looking at the floor, except Mr. Congo; he kept looking straight at Mr. Hodges with a defiant grin on his face.

It seemed like minutes before Mr. Hodges said, "Coach, would you mind coming over here?"

Jerry walked over and stood beside him.

"Do you see that big fellow sitting in the middle of that group of boys?"

"Yes sir, I do."

"Would you mind stepping out in the hall with that gentleman and having a talk with him?"

"No sir. I would enjoy talking with him."

Mr. Hodges motioned for the boy to come on down. Some of the other students began to snicker and a slight murmur made a wave across the rest of the students. After a long pause, Gongo began to slowly rise to his feet and amble down to where Mr. Hodges and the coach were standing.

Mr. Hodges then turned to Jerry and in a low voice, said, "Remember what you told me about how you handled certain situations?"

"Yes sir, I certainly do."

"This is one of them."

Jerry reached up to Congo, placing his right hand on the outside of the boy's right upper arm and his left hand on the inside of the boy's arm. He then clamped the loose skin on the inside of Congo's arm between his four finger tips and

Carl Otto

the palm of his hand, The boy started to pull away, but as he did the new coach whispered, "Don't struggle unless you want to lose a big chunk of your arm."

A look of confusion came over Congo's face and the smirk disappeared.

"Now, lets you and me take a little walk."

Again he started to pull away, but with every slight escape move he made Jerry clamped down more. The inside of the arm is very sensitive to pain, when pinched. The boy soon realized this new coach had a grip like a vice. Jerry started leading the young man toward the door and out into the hall, shutting the door as they exited.

"That hurts." Congo said, as they went into the hall.

"You bet it hurts. And let me tell you something else; I know ways to hurt a smart alex like you like you cannot imagine."

Jerry released his grip and as soon as it was free, the boy placed the palm of his hand on Jerry's chest and started to shove, saying, "&%$#$%— you, you little %$@*&%."

He never finished his remark because the coach immediately placed his right hand on top of the boy's hand, holding it tight against his own chest. With the other hand, he grasped the boy's elbow of that same arm and began bending the boy's wrist, forcing him to his knees.

"Oh. So now you want to get foul mouthed, do you?"

Before Congo realized what was happening, he was

Congo and Samantha

down on his knees and the coach had him in a hold from which he could not escape.

"You're hurting my arm."

"What is it going take to convince you that you are not in my league? Is foul language the best you can do? You had better get it through that thick skull of yours that you are not messing with one of your buddies. You are messing with an Army veteran who has been trained to kill with his bare hands. I was spending three months of combat during the war while you were practicing the art of popping pimples."

Jerry released Congo and allowed him to stand. As he rose to a standing position, he said, "You have convinced me Coach."

"Good! Now let's go back in the auditorium with the rest of the group. Just walk back through that door and go seat yourself as if nothing has taken place, Okay."

He told Congo to go in first and he followed.

As he walked up to Mr. Hodges, the principal asked, "Did you and Congo get everything straightened out?"

"Yes sir, we sure did. We had a nice talk and I think we understand each other, isn't that right Congo?"

"You bet we do, Coach."

"What did you talk about?"

"Well, actually sir, it was kind of private. We would like to keep it between the two of us, right Congo?"

Carl Otto

"Just between the two of us. That's right Coach."

Jerry never had another ounce of trouble with that boy, or any of the other kids, because he knew how to handle situations such as that; as a matter of fact Congo and the coach became close friends. He did have another problem develop; one he had never anticipated and also one for which he had absolutely no training.

One of his professors had warned Jerry and his classmates to be alert to a fact that young high school girls and boys develop crushes on young male and female teachers. He also told them, "They will get crushes on married teachers too, but single teachers are more apt to yield to the temptation. DON'T do it! It will come back and bite you in the rear real hard."

Jerry could see his professor's point. Obviously a single handsome hunk could be faced with that problem, but he thought, "I can see his point if a guy is a handsome dude, but a short ordinary guy like me will never have to worry about it."

Jerry was wrong.

The school year was well into the first nine weeks when Gongo approached the coach one day.

"Coach, I need to talk to you sometime."

"Any time Congo. What is your problem?"

"It ain't my problem Coach."

"Oh? Whose problem is it?"

Congo and Samantha

"It's yours."

"Mine! What are you getting at?"

"All I can say right now, is it concerns you and one of the girls."

"You're pulling my leg Congo."

He slowly moved his head back and forth.

"You are serious, aren't you?"

"Dead serious."

"Who in the world is it?"

"I gotta go to class right now. I'll see ya later."

Jerry's next assignment was study hall supervision. He met in the Library with a small group of mixed sophomores and juniors. The kids seated themselves around the library tables and he helped them with assignments if they needed assistance.

He was thinking, "I can't imagine him telling me something like that as a way to get even with me for that first day incident. No, he wouldn't do that. He is the first baseman and clean-up hitter on the baseball team. I couldn't ask for a better kid. Oh, he back-slides once in awhile, in Lidia's class, but she has trouble with half the kids."

Jerry met Congo in the hall, between classes, and stopped him.

"Say Congo, I have an old movie that features Lou Gehrig playing first base. I'd like you to come over tonight and see it. I think you can learn from it."

201

Carl Otto

"What time do you want me there, Coach?"

"How about seven?"

"I'll be there."

The coach was practically paranoid before the day was over. Every time a girl smiled at him, he would think, "I she the one?"

That was a long day.

Congo came by the boarding house a little before seven. Jerry walked out to the pick-up and said, "This situation has had me stewing all day long. Now tell be about it."

"Well Coach, I had a date with Alice last week end, and she told me Samantha told her, that you and her have been makin out."

"Samantha told Alice I have been making out with her!"

"Yep. That's what Alice told me."

"Oh for crying out loud!" Jerry paced back and forth as he removed his cap and slapped the side of his leg with it.

"Did Alice believe her?"

"Well, you are single. And if you have a girl, nobody knows about it."

"Congo, do you believe it?"

"Is it true, Coach?"

"Of course it's not true!"

Jerry just walked in a circle for a moment.

Then he said, "Congo, I can't thank you enough for tell-

202

Congo and Samantha

ing me about this. This is the kind of thing that could ruin my career before it hardly gets started."

"I really didn't think you was guilty; that's why I come and told ya."

"Have you told anyone else about this?"

"I told Ted, and we talked about it. We decided it was a bunch of bull. Ted also thought I should tell you."

Jerry just leaned on Congo's truck for a moment. "Congo, this thing is only a rumor; I have never treated Samantha any differently than I have any of the rest of the girls. But it is a rumor I must get stopped, right now. Do you know where Samantha lives?"

"Yes I do, why?"

"Because I am going to her place right now and have a talk with that little lady."

"Would you like to have me go over there with you?"

"Would you do that for me?"

"Yeah I would. Hop in, I'll drive you out there right now."

Jerry got in Congo's pickup and he drove out in the country about three miles to Samantha's home.

Jerry said, "Maybe you should stay in the truck. I don't want to involve you if it is not necessary."

He walked to the front door and knocked. Samantha answered the door. Jerry never saw a kid with a more shocked look on her face.

203

Carl Otto

"Good evening Samantha, may I come in?"

She stood frozen in her tracks, but her mother appeared behind her. "Hi Coach, what brings you out here this evening?"

"I think Samantha might have something to tell you. Is her dad here?"

"Samantha began crying and ran for her room."

"What is going on here Coach?"

"We have a little problem that has developed; it concerns Samantha."

"Pray tell, what is it?"

"I think it would better if Samantha told you."

Her mother went directly to Samantha's room. She was lying on the bed, crying. Her dad appeared as they were going in the bedroom.

"What in the world is going on here?"

"Coach tells me Samantha has something to tell us."

Her dad walked to her bed, grasped her by an arm and pulled her to her feet, "Ok Sammie, why are you crying?"

"Well Daddy, I was just kidding about something, and somebody took it serious."

Her mother stepped directly in front of her, grasped her shoulders with both hands and said, "Samantha. Just exactly what were you kidding about?"

"Well - - ah - - em - - - - -I sort of - - told Alice that - - ah

Congo and Samantha

- - that - - me and Coach - Couch were - - kinda - - having an affair."

A low growl came from her dad. "This better not be true."

Jerry spoke up, "Believe me, Mr. Edwards, it is not true."

"I was just kidding around, Daddy. Nothing ever happened."

"Sammie, I ought to take my belt off and tan your butt until you can't sit down."

"That would not solve the problem, Mr. Edwards."

"She has to be punished."

"Sir, I think she is being punished right now. Do you folks mind if I have a one on one talk with Samantha."

They looked at each other for a moment, and then nodded their approval. They left the room and shut the door as they went out.

Jerry sat down beside Samantha. "Have I given you cause to think what you were kidding about, would be possible?"

"No."

"Have you told anyone besides Alice?"

"No. Just Alice."

"Do you have a reason for doing this?"

"Well, Alice is always bragging about how many boys she can have. She says all she has to do is snap her fingers and they come running."

"And you think that makes Alice better than you?"

"Well, no boys are interested in me."

205

Carl Otto

"Oh Samantha, you are only a sophomore. You are not yet fully developed. You are just as pretty and just as desirable as any girl in school. You don't have to make up tales."

"You really think so Coach?"

"I am certain of it, but you do realize how serious this thing could be? I could get fired from my job. A false rumor, such as this one, could really hurt my reputation. It could also be a bad thing for your own reputation."

"I know Coach, I am so sorry I did it. I just never thought before I spouted off."

"Samantha, this incident reminds me of a story I once heard about a person who had been gossiping about others. It seems the person began to realize the gossiping was wrong, and so the individual went to the Priest and confessed about the gossiping."

The Priest listened carefully and thought for a moment before he said, "For your penance I want you to go place a feather on the doorstep of everyone about whom you have gossiped, and then come back to me when you are finished."

So the individual went to every doorstep and placed a feather, as the Priest had directed. The gossiper then went back to the Priest.

"Father, I have done as you told me to do."

The Priest then said, "Now go back to all those doorsteps and get those feathers. Bring them back to me."

Congo and Samantha

The gossiper was confused. After a moment the Priest said, "Of course you could not go back and retrieve the feathers; they have blown all over town by the wind. So it is with a rumor."

Samatha looked at the coach for a long moment, then bowed her head and said, "Oh my Coach, do you think it is too late for me to 'gather up the feathers?'"

"No Samanta. We are fortunate to live in a small town. I think you will be able to gather up the feathers."

"I hope you are right, Coach."

"And what are you going to do about it?"

"First off, I will never ever do something like that again. And I am going to tell Alice and anyone else who knows about it that I was just kidding around. I really am sorry Coach."

"Sounds to me like you have the problem solved. Let's go tell your folks."

They went into the living room and told her parents about their conversation. Her dad still thought she deserved a good "whippin," but he also agreed she probably learned a lesson that she would never forget. So they left it at that. Jerry went out to the pickup and joined Congo.

On the way back to town, Jerry told Congo everything that had taken place while he was waiting. As he finished telling the details, Congo slowed down and pulled into a field driveway.

"Why are you stopping?"

"Coach, you mentioned she said no boys were ever interested in her."

"Yes, she said that."

"Well, I have an idea. We have that fall Prom coming up next month, and I don't have a date. I asked Alice, but she said she was goin with Fred, so I am going to go back there and ask Samantha if she would like to go to it with me."

"You are going back there right now?"

"Yep. I am. The way I figure it, if I tell her that on the first day of school, you taught me a lesson I will never forget. And, then tonight you have taught her a lesson she will nev-

Congo and Samantha

er forget, she ought to think we're supposed to go together."

"Congo, you are about to make me cry."

He drove back to the Edwards place, got out of the truck and went to the door. Mr. Edwards answered the door and they both went inside. He was there not more than ten minutes when he came running back to his truck. He was grinning from ear to ear.

"She liked the idea, and so did her mom and dad."

There are special times in our lives, and there are very special times in our lives; it is not difficult to identify one of those very special times when it comes along.

THE END

UNCLE CHARLIE
IS A ROUNDER

UNCLE CHARLIE IS A ROUNDER

The school term of 1943 has just ended and Paul Saker is getting ready to do something he knows his mom thinks he shouldn't be doing, but he will be seventeen years old in August and feels he just can't pass up a chance to have a good steady job that will last all summer long.

He is thinking, "I know that Mom thinks uncle Charlie is a rounder, and I suppose she is right. After all, he is forty-three years old and he has been married three times already. Dad says the best thing about uncle Charlie is that he is "shootin blanks." None of his three ex wives ever had any kids while they were married to him. Maybe that is better for all concerned."

Paul's problem was, his uncle Charlie came through town last month and stayed a few days with them, and while he was there, he told Paul if he would come to Oklahoma City, as soon as school is out, he would get him a job with the construction company where he works .

The job would be working on building Tinker Air Force Base. He said the pay would be at least $.75 an hour, plus overtime.

Last summer Paul worked at Mack's Garage for thirty-five cents an hour, and he didn't get any overtime. So, for the first time in his life he could be making "big" money, and for the first time in his life he is going against his parents advise,

213

Carl Otto

He told his Mom and Dad that he was going take Uncle Charlie up on his offer.

Paul's Mom finally said he could go, but she told him, "You find a place to live by yourself, and you do not run around with Charlie. I repeat, you do not run around with Charlie."

Paul promised her he would get a room by myself and that he would not run around with Uncle Charlie.

World War II was in full bloom, so Paul knew he would probably be going into some branch of the service in another year or so. He has finished his sophomore year in high school. He has $172 dollars saved up, so that should let him get by until he gets his first paycheck.

School was out during the last week of May in 1943. Paul boarded a bus in Columbus, Kansas the next day and was on his way to Oklahoma City. Uncle Charlie gave him an address and a phone number where he could find him, so he was all set. His heart was beating so fast he thought it was going to jump out of his chest.

Paul soon found out how green he was. Just by chance, he sat in the seat next to an old man who asked him where he was going. Paul was glad to hear the old fellow was also going to Oklahoma City, because they had to make three bus changes before they got there, so Paul stuck to that old man like he was flypaper. The old fellow also had a daughter who was meeting him at the bus station. He knew Oklahoma

Uncle Charlie Is A Rounder

City like the back of his hand, so he told Paul about a good boarding house where he could rent a room at a reasonable price. And, he had his daughter drop Paul off at that boarding house. The time was 3:p.m. on Saturday afternoon.

The sign in front of the boarding house was plainly printed, "ROOM AND BOARD $10 PER WEEK (Without meals - $5) Paul was a green country kid, so he was wondering, "Does room and Board mean you have to sleep on a board?"

The sign was printed black on white, except for the large red letters, NO COLORED. He walked in the front door and into a foyer. Another sign read, "Ring for Service." He pushed the bell button.

After several minutes, a little plump gray haired lady came out one of the doors.

"Would you like a room Sonny?"

"Yes'm, I would."

"Step in here" She motioned to the room she had just come from.

The room looked like any living room in almost any house.

"What is your name Son?"

"Paul Saker."

"I am Mrs. Rabilia, but everybody calls me Granny. I am the chief cook and bottle washer around here, so if you have any questions, you come to me."

215

Carl Otto

She continued, "Do you want room and board, or do you just want a room?"

"Well, I'm new around here, so I don't know anything about the town. What do you think I should do?"

"I think you should take room and board. That would include a room and two meals each day; breakfast and supper; you're on your own for lunch."

"So, the 'ROOM' part of Room and Board, means meals?"

She chuckled a little as she answered, "Yes, the board part means meals; the room part means a bed and a place to keep your stuff."

"Okay, then I'll take them both."

"Good. That will be four weeks in advance."

Paul gave her three tens and two fives and she said, "Follow me."

As they headed for his room she explained that the women renters occupied the first floor, except for her own three-roomed apartment, and the men and married couples occupied the second floor. The dining room was in the basement and there was a bathroom on each floor. The men shared the bathroom on the second floor and the women shared the bathroom on the first floor. Anybody could use the one under the stairway that leads to the basement.

"Right now, I have only one married couple, and I do not allow children or pets. I have a cat, and I don't want her dis-

Uncle Charlie Is A Rounder

turbed by other pets. All my renters must be at least sixteen years old. How old are you?"

"I was sixteen last August."

"You don't look it, but I'll take your word for it. Here is your room."

"The room was adequate sized; there was a three-quarter bed, a chest of drawers, a small table and two straight back wooden chairs. On one wall was a small lavatory with a mirror above.

"How does this look to you?"

"It looks fine to me."

"You will get clean sheets once a week."

She gestured toward the small lavatory as she said, "And, this thing is not a urinal!"

Paul had to chuckle at that last remark, but he knew she was serious.

As she left, she said, "Good to have you Paul. The meal schedule and times are posted on the kitchen door by the dining room. You might want to go check them out."

After he put his few things away, he counted his money. He still had $109.12. He went back down to the owner's quarters and knocked on her door.

"You already have a question?"

"I have an Uncle who lives in this town, and I need to get in touch with him. I don't know how to do it."

"Do you have an address?"

217

Carl Otto

"Yes. And a telephone number."

"Well, come on in. We will try to call him."

Mrs. Rabilia made the phone call. While she was making the call, her cat started rubbing on Paul's leg and purring.

"What's her name?"

"Queenie, cause she's the queen of the house."

When Uncle Charlie answered, she handed Paul the phone.

"Hi Uncle Charlie. I'm here."

"Who is this?"

"This is your nephew, Paul."

"Paul. Where'd you say you are?"

"Here in Oklahoma City."

" What are you doing down here?"

"I'm here because you told me to come."

"I did? I don't remember telling you to come down here."

"Uncle Charlie; you told me to come down here as soon as school was out. You said you would have a job for me."

Then he said, "Where are you? I'll come get you and we'll go out and eat supper together."

"I'm at a boarding house; you can pick me up here."

Mrs. Rabilia took the phone. "I'll tell him where to pick you up."

She told Uncle Charlie, "Okay, he'll be waiting out front."

It was almost five before Charlie showed up. Paul went out to his car where his uncle introduced him to some

218

Uncle Charlie Is A Rounder

woman that looked like what his mom would call, "a Real Floozie."

"This is my nephew, Paul. Paul, this is Trixie."

Paul thought, "Wow! Mom, if you was here you would say her name fits her looks."

"Hi Trixie."

Charlie told him that he and Trixie were just getting ready to "go out on the town" and if he wanted to join them, he was welcome.

Paul told them he thought he would stay here and get settled in. Then he asked, "What about that job you told me was waiting for me?"

"Oh, I forgot about that."

He continued, "Heck, I don't work out there anymore."

Carl Otto

Paul could smell liquor fumes coming out of the car, so he quickly realized Uncle Charlie was just exactly what his mom said he was. He was indeed a Rounder.

Paul stepped back from the car and said, "It's just as well, Uncle Charlie, cause I found a different job just this morning. So, you and Trixie go ahead out on the town, I'll see ya later."

"Okay, good to see ya Paul."

"Nice to meet you Paul."

"You too Trixie."

They sped off and Paul turned slowly back toward the boarding house. He must have had a droopy look as he went up those front steps.

"Hey boy, you've got a face long enough to eat oats out of a churn."

He looked up to see Mrs. Rabilia standing at the top of the stairs.

"I didn't like the tone of that man's voice when I talked to him on the phone. My advise is to stay away from him."

She motioned toward the porch swing, and they sat down. Paul told her all about how his Uncle had enticed him into coming down to Oklahoma City, telling him he would get him a job out at Tinker.

"You know something Paul, you came to the right place when you rented a room here."

"What do you mean?"

220

Uncle Charlie Is A Rounder

"I mean my oldest son is a foreman for one of the construction companies out there, and I'll just bet my britches that he can get you a job."

"Are you serious?"

"I most certainly am. I will give him a call this very evening."

Paul felt like a ton of weight had been lifted off his shoulders.

"Thanks a lot Mrs. Rabilia."

"Incidentally Paul, remember that most of the roomers here call me Granny. So, I want you to call me Granny too, OK?"

"I like Granny, cause you make me think about my own Grandma Saker."

She slapped Paul on the knee as she stood erect, "We start serving supper at 6p.m. so be sure to be there."

He went back up to his room and on the way he noticed that all the rooms have screen doors on the side toward the hall and regular doors that opened inside. He also noticed there was a steady breeze in the hallway.

He really didn't look the room over very good when Granny showed it to him, but now he was checking it out good. First thing he noticed was no breeze. The air was still and hot. So he opened the window and as soon as he cracked it a few inches the wind started blowing in. He later learned

221

Carl Otto

there was a great big exhaust fan up in the attic that kept the air moving, and that Granny called it the air-conditioner,

It was getting close to six o'clock, so he went down to the basement. The entire basement was nothing but kitchen and a food storage area and a dining room that had the biggest table Paul had ever seen.

He thought, "Wow, the kitchen table at Brownells, back home, is big enough for all their ten kids to sit around, but this one looks like it could seat an army."

In that large room, there was just that one big table and probably twenty chairs at one end and a kitchen in the other end.

Back at the big kitchen stove, there was a colored lady who seemed to be the cook. When Paul saw her, he thought, "Hmmm, the sign out front said "No Colored," but here is a colored lady in the kitchen."

Then he noticed two girls, who looked about his age, by a great big three compartment sink, washing dishes. He was glad to see he wasn't the only kid there.

It wasn't quite six, but it was plain to see that supper was almost ready. Paul went in and seated myself at the table. When the cook and the girls started putting bowls of food on the table, one of the girls leaned over to him.

"You're supposed to get your own plate and silverware over there." She pointed to a table in the corner.

Then she added, "They have the best meals you ever

Uncle Charlie Is A Rounder

tasted here; Mrs. Chauncy is really a good cook; in fact she is really a nice old lady. We all love her."

People started coming in, picking up plates and silverware and sitting around the table. Paul was really hungry because all he had eaten so far the whole day was a light breakfast and a candy bar. The big bowls in the middle of the table had mashed potatoes, gravy, green beans and corn. While he was dishing up helpings of the staples, one of those girls came over and forked a pork chop out of a big skillet into his plate.

"You get to eat all you can hold of the food in the bowls, but you get just one pork chop."

"Do you work here all the time?"

"No, me and Marsha work at a laundry on week days, but we work here on Saturday and Sunday. My name is Betty, What's yours?"

"Paul."

"Where ya from?"

"Southeast Kansas."

"Where do ya work?"

"I just got here this afternoon, so I ain't got a job yet."

"You won't have any trouble finding a job, if you really want to work, because this town has lots of jobs available."

"My uncle had me come down here - - ." He didn't get finished telling her his story because she had to get back to her job.

223

Carl Otto

She said, "I gotta get to work; maybe I'll see ya later."

Paul answered a sheepish, "Okay."

Like any normal sixteen year old boy, Paul liked girls, but he was real bad at trying to talk to one; he certainly was not bashful at eating mashed potatoes and gravy, green beans and corn, and one porkchop. He was really shoveling it in when Betty came over to him.

"Would you like a glass of milk or iced tea or water?

"Yes, I would."

"Do you want all three or just one of them?"

"Oh, I'm sorry. Just milk I guess."

She walked over to a table where there were several pitchers of drinks and a big coffee urn. Paul noticed when she poured the milk into that the table contained a tray of glasses and a tray of coffee cups.

"I was supposed to get my own drink, wasn't I?"

"Yes, but since you are new, I'll do it this time."

"Thanks a lot."

She placed her hand on his shoulder as she set the glass by his plate, gave his shoulder a little squeeze and said, "No problem Paul, maybe you can do something for me sometime."

He looked up into her smiling face. "I hope so."

Then he continued, "Can I ask you something?"

"Sure. What do you want to know."

"Well, when I came here this afternoon, I noticed a sign

Uncle Charlie Is A Rounder

that said, 'No Colored.' Yet there is a colored lady doing the cookin. Does she live here?"

"No. It ain't allowed down here."

"What do you mean; it ain't allowed?"

As she headed back to her work, she said, "This is the south ya know."

He went back up to his room with a very full stomach, but he also had a lot of things buzzing around in his head.

He was thinking, "That Betty is not a very pretty girl, or at least she ain't according to the standards I have always set. She ain't the cheerleader type, or the homecoming queen type. She fits into the category I always called, a farmers daughter. But she has a very nice voice; she has a pleasant smile; she is clean and she smells good. Maybe the reason I have trouble talking to girls is due more to the kind of girl I always want to talk to. Betty seemed to want to talk to me. Maybe some of those girls back home are really not my type. Come to think of it, that girl is the first one that ever acted like she might be interested in me. Hmmmm. And, what did she mean by, 'this is the south ya know?'"

Paul was also thinking about what Granny had told him about her grandson. "I sure hope she ain't a spoofing me."

He didn't have to consider Granny's son very long because while he was stretched out on the bed, he heard Granny call to me, "Paul, come on down here. I got somebody I want you to meet."

225

Carl Otto

He hurried down the stairs and down the hall to Granny's apartment; she was standing in the door. As he reached the door, she placed her hand on his shoulder and said, "Eldon, this is the lad I was telling you about."

He extended his hand. "Eldon Mason, and you are?"

"I'm Paul Saker."

"Do you have any working experience, Paul?"

"Yes Sir, I worked in a garage all last summer. And I have done painting and lots of stuff."

"Do you think you could handle a job as an oiler on a dragline?"

"You bet I could. That's the kind of stuff I did for Mack Heimrick last summer."

"Well, we have an Oiler job open. You could start working Monday morning."

"Really! No kidding, you do have a job for me?"

He smiled and answered, "Yes, Son, I do have a job for you. Do you want it?"

Paul said, "Great! You bet, I'll take it."

"Aren't you gonna ask how much it pays?"

"Well Sir, I figure it will pay a fair wage. I am just happy to get the job."

"Good. I will be by here at 6a.m. Monday morning. I will take you to work the first day. Then you can learn about the bus schedules and bus stops later."

226

Uncle Charlie Is A Rounder

"Gee, that's awful nice of ya. Gee thanks. Golly, thanks a lot."

He took a deep breath and exhaled with an almost whistling sound. "Gee I'm glad to get a job."

He turned to Granny. "Oh thanks Granny. I don't know what I would have done without you."

He went to her and gave her a big hug.

Then he turned to Eldon. "You won't regret giving me a chance. I guarantee I'm a good worker."

He went back upstairs to his room. When he got there, a boy who looked about his age, greeted him.

"Hi, my name is Fred Jones. I understand you are new around here."

"Yeah, I just got here today. My name is Paul Saker."

"Marsha told me about you."

"Marsha?"

"Yeah, Marsha. She is one of the girls who works in the kitchen. Mary's the other."

"Oh yeah, Marsha. Betty told me the other girl was named Marsha, but I never actually met her."

"Hi Paul, good to meet you. The reason I'm here now, is Marsha and I are going to a show tonite. Betty is coming with us, and we wondered if you would like to join us."

"Yeah, of course I would. Does Betty know you are asking me?"

"Hey Buddy, she suggested it."

Carl Otto

"Wow! Sure, I'd love to go. When are you leaving?"

"As soon as the girls get off working in the kitchen."

"Would that give me enough time to take a shower?"

"I think so, but make it a quick one."

Paul grabbed a clean pair of jeans and a T shirt and headed for the bathroom. He set a record in taking a shower. Granny had told him not to take too long anytime he had to go to the bathroom, but he don't think anyone will ever have to wait on him long, if he keeps up that pace.

Only thing wrong, he forgot to bring any clean briefs with him to the bathroom. So he put his jeans on right quick and started for his room. Fred was waiting for him at the door.

"Come on, the girls are waiting downstairs."

It was a good thing he had a crew-cut, cause he sure didn't have time to comb his hair. He slipped his T shirt on, jammed his sockless feet into his penny loafers, pulled his bedroom door shut and headed down the stairs after Fred. The girls were waiting for them by the back door.

They walked about four blocks to a bus stop. As they approached the bus stop, Paul realized he had forgotten his wallet. He didn't even have a penny with him.

"Oh dad blast it, Oh dad-gum it, I was hurrying so fast I forgot to bring my money. Oh heck, I can't go. You guys go ahead, I'll have to go back."

Uncle Charlie Is A Rounder

Betty grabbed his hand and said, "No you are not. I have enough money for both of us. It'll be my treat, tonight."

"Oh Betty. That ain't right. I bet you guys thought I forgot my money on purpose."

They all three answered at the same time, "No we didn't."

"But is my money safe there? I didn't lock the door when I hurried out."

Betty answered, "Yes, your money is safe. We never have a problem like that at Granny's."

"I'll tell you what I'll do, Paul." Fred suggested, "I'll loan you five bucks right now, and you can pay me back six dollars when we get back to the boarding house later tonight."

Betty gave him a shove. "Indeed you will not! Paul is my date tonight, and you are not gonna be a loan shark."

The bus was rolling to a stop. Betty took his hand and started pulling him toward the bus.

She said, "The bus ride is a dime and the show is fifty cents; popcorn and pop are ten cents each. Come on, you're in good hands."

They rode the city bus for a couple of miles before it stopped one/half block from a theater. Betty bought tickets for herself and Paul. When they got into the lobby, she bought two sacks of popcorn and two bottles of NuGrape. The newsreel was playing as they looked for seats. They could not find four seats together, so Marsha and Fred went

Carl Otto

further down front. Betty and Paul seated themselves near the back.

Mary patted Paul's hand and said, "Stop worrying. It's okay. You get to pay from now on, every time we go out. Okay?"

"Alright. You do make me feel a lot better."

After they were seated a few minutes, the realization began to hit Paul that he did not have his briefs on. He thought, "Oh gosh! Dad used to say that a guy who wore overalls and no shorts was a swinger. I guess it applies to jeans and no shorts too. Only difference is; jeans are a lot tighter than overalls."

He began to get "pinched" in places he could not adjust at the moment. He squirmed a little, but the pinches were only worse.

He was thinking, "Oh, if I could only stand up for a second."

He had no idea what the newsreel was about. He was trying to get his hand in his pocket, but when you're wearing a pair of tight fitting jeans, that doesn't work when you're sitting. It seemed that every breath he took was pulling and pinching got worse.

He began to remember other things too; like his grandpa telling about the stingy man who wanted to buy his boy something to wear and something to play with, so he just bought him a pair of pants and cut one front pocket out

230

Uncle Charlie Is A Rounder

of them. He thought, "I wish I had a hole in my pocket big enough to get my hand in."

Finally, Betty whispered, "Are you alright?"

"I'm fine." He whispered back.

"No you're not. Is it me?"

"Oh no Betty, it's not you."

"Well then, what is it?"

He thought, "Oh Holy Cow! I can't let her think I don't like being with her."

He also remembered his mom telling him many times, "Honesty is the best policy."

So he motioned for her to lean closer, and then he whispered in her ear, "I didn't have time to put on any shorts, and I'm getting pinched – big time."

She turned facing him and whispered loudly, "You don't have any shorts on?"

"Shhhhh, not so loud."

Then she started giggling. "I can't help it - it's funny."

Paul heard someone behind them say, "He forgot to put his shorts on, and now he's getting pinched."

Then some guy said right out loud, "For crying out loud kid, stand up and make an adjustment."

Betty, and everybody around them, were laughing so hard they could hardly breathe.

So, he just did what the guy suggested. He stood up, put

231

Carl Otto

his hand down the front of his jeans, made the adjustment and sat down.

Finally the laughter subsided. But it didn't last long. Betty asked him, "Are you gonna eat your popcorn with that hand?"

She started laughing again. At least the cartoon was playing, so most everyone thought Loony Tunes was getting the laughter.

He leaned over to Betty and said, "I took a shower, so my hand is clean."

When the movie ended and the four of them met in the lobby, Marsha asked, "Do you guys know what was causing all the confusion during the cartoon?"

Betty got tickled again, and Paul got tickled. Then Fred and Marsha insisted they tell them what was so funny. Betty could hardly stop laughing long enough to tell the story, but she didn't tell it exactly as it happened.

She said, "Some guy behind us forgot to put on his shorts before he left home and his tight jeans started pinching him, so he was squirming around until his wife asked him what was the matter; he told her loud enough that we all heard. Then another guy told him to stand up and make an adjustment, so he did, and everybody laughed."

Paul leaned close to Betty and said, "Thanks, I'll never ever forget you for that."

She just squeezed his hand.

232

Uncle Charlie Is A Rounder

They were on the city bus when Betty told the story and the driver and all the passengers must have thought they were drunk.

Paul knew one thing for certain; if laughter is the best medicine, they all got a good dose of good medicine that night.

Paul went to work at his new job on Monday morning. He really liked the man who was the operator of the dragline on which he worked. He also discovered he could work a lot of overtime as a Mechanic's Helper. The company had a big shop where about five mechanics worked, and they were always in need of someone to help them. They especially like Paul because he knew all about tools and wrench sizes and stuff like that. So if one of them said, "Hey Kid, bring me a 5/8-3/4 box end," He knew what was wanted.

So at $.75 regular time, $1.03 overtime and $1.50 on Sundays, Paul was really making big money. And, since the building of Tinker Air Force Base was a high priority job, the work went on twenty-four hours a day, seven days a week. He got paid every two weeks and his first paycheck was almost a hundred dollars. Uncle Charlie must have known when his first payday came around, because he showed up at Granny's that evening wanting to borrow some money. Paul lied to him; he told him I had sent it all home.

The only bad thing about working overtime was he didn't get to see much of Mary. She and Marsha worked at

Carl Otto

a laundry and, due to the extreme summer heat, along with no air-conditioning, they had to go to work at four in the morning; by afternoon, it was so hot in that laundry, they couldn't work. So those two girls worked from four a.m. until one o'clock in the afternoon.

Almost every day the girls were already in bed sleeping by the time Paul got home from work. He did have a number of chances to visit with Mary between the times he got home from work and she had to get to bed, but their opportunities to date were not as often as he would have liked.

Fred and Paul went to a movie once in awhile, but there were only three other times that he got to take Mary out on a date since their working hours didn't jive. All three times came when a rain that made a big mud hole out of Paul's worksite and the mechanics had time to get caught up with their work, so they didn't need a helper.

The last time he got to leave Tinker early, he was back at the boarding house in time to eat supper with Fred, Marsha and Mary. And, they decided to go to the Skating Rink; they didn't have time for a movie because the girls had to get to sleep early.

Paul always remembered how impressed he was when he found out how good Mary could skate. She could skate backwards as fast as she could go forward. And, she could do spins and leg lifts and a lot of stuff. She taught Paul how

Uncle Charlie Is A Rounder

to hold her hands and then do real fast spins. He got dizzy and fell most of the time, but she never did fall.

And they did a lot of couples skating. Sometimes, Paul skated with Marsha and Fred skated with Mary, but most of the time Mary and Paul were together. He was beginning to really like her. She was always so neat and clean. She didn't wear a lot of fancy smelling perfume; she just smelled good. She had real pretty wavy dark brown hair, her eyes were the darkest blue he had ever seen, her teeth were a little bit crooked, but not enough to spoil her smile. She was really a neat person.

Paul got to thinking, "I ain't never kissed a girl, but I sure would like to try it on Mary"

He was too green to realize it at the time how much she was attracted to him. Even on the evening of one of his dates with her, as they were walking back to the boarding house, and she and Paul were strolling about fifteen feet behind Fred and Marsha, she said, "Let's ditch those two."

She grabbed him be the hand and pulled him into an alley. She said, "Let's hide in this doorway and see how long it takes them to realize we're gone."

So the two of them stepped back into this partially darkened doorway and they stood face to face for a long moment. She gave him a perfect opportunity, and he was too bashful to take advantage of the situation. Paul didn't realize it, but she knew he was not rejecting her. She was

Carl Otto

aware he did like her; she knew he was bashful and timid around girls.

Back in his room later he was reprimanding himself; he knew he had missed his golden opportunity; however, he did vow that next time they went on a date, he was going to kiss that girl.

It was two weeks before they had an opportunity to go out again, and as before, they went to the skating rink. They were having a great time when for some reason the two girls had a disagreement about something. Neither Fred nor Paul ever knew what it was all about, but the two girls nearly came to blows. After one of their short exchanges of words, Mary went to remove her skates. Paul followed her.

He asked, "Is there anything I can do?"

"No. You just as well stay here and skate. I'm going home."

He answered, "I don't want to stay without you, Mary."

He held her hand as they walked back to the boarding house without much talk and when they arrived she turned to him and said, "It had nothing to do with you, because I really like you. It was strictly Marsha."

She then leaned forward and kissed him goodnight and went to her room.

Paul was one confused kid. He had just been kissed for the first time. And, by a girl he was really beginning to like.

Uncle Charlie Is A Rounder

He was worried about the fight she and her friend had. It took him a long time to fall asleep.

Paul was sound asleep at around three-thirty in the early morning, when he heard a knock on his door. He got out of bed and went to the door. Marsha was standing there, barefoot and in her slip; she was crying and she was almost hysterical.

She grabbed Paul's hand and said, "Something is terribly wrong with Mary."

Paul hurried down the stairs with Marsha and they went directly to the bathroom. Mary was on her back in the dry bathtub. All she was wearing were her panties and her slip, and, something was definitely wrong. She was grunting and groaning, and seemed to be choking on her own tongue. She did not respond to anything they asked her. She was kicking the metal faucets and the tub spout with her bare feet, she was bumping her head on the tub and thrashing her arms and hands around; she was bleeding from the mouth and from several spots on her feet and ankles.

Paul didn't know what to do, but he knew she had to be taken out of that tub. He leaned over and worked his arms under her twisting, shaking, convulsing body and just smothered her arms against his chest with his two arms. He stood her up and then put his right arm under her legs, pulling her body up into his arms. Holding her tightly, he carried her thrashing body into her bedroom and placed her on her

237

Carl Otto

stomach on the bed; she was still convulsing. So Fred, who had arrived by then, and Paul got on the two sides of the bed and held a sheet tightly over her while Marsha went to get a nurse who was also living in the boarding house

The nurse was there in only a few minutes; she told them what was wrong with Mary. Suddenly Paul realized he was standing in the presence of the nurse, Marsha and Fred with only his jockey shorts on. His hands and arms, as well as his chest, shorts and legs were splotched with Mary's blood.

Uncle Charlie Is A Rounder

The nurse said to him, "You just as well go get cleaned up. She will be okay, but she will sleep for a while. These seizures are very exhausting."

Paul went to his room where he took a wet washcloth and removed all the blood from himself and changed shorts. He lay back down on his bed, but he was unable to go back to sleep. Paul had never seen a person have a seizure before, and Now he had just observed a young girl, whom he was beginning to really like a lot, have a real serious one.

He thought about Mary for the rest of the day and the instant he got back to the boarding house from his job site, he began looking for her. She was not in her room, nor was Marsha, so he went to Granny. She told him Mary's parents came and got her earlier in the day.

"When will she be back?"

"Paul, they took all her belongings and moved her out this afternoon; she will not be coming back."

"She won't?"

"You really like that girl, don't you?"

"I guess I do. I never got to know her real good, but I do like her. And, I have been feeling sorry for her and worrying about her all day. Do you know if Marsha is still here?"

"Marsha moved out this morning while Mary was still sleeping. She called some of her people, and they picked her up about nine o'clock. Do you know what those girls were fighting about?"

Carl Otto

"No. Fred and I never knew what it was about. But they started arguing when we were at the skating rink. Mary finally said she had enough and started to leave. I walked back here with her, but she never would say what it was about; she just told me it had nothing to do with me."

Granny said, "I think I know without knowing. Mary was always the one who paid their rent money. They worked out their meals bill, but I think Mary might have even loaned Marsha some money one time too."

Paul mused, "Ah-huh. I'll bet you're right. It seemed like any time the girls paid for anything, is was Mary who did the paying."

"You know the old saying? Money is the root of all evil."

"Granny, do you reckon that getting mad and all upset like she was, is what caused her to have that fit?"

"It was a seizure, Paul; a Grand Mal Seizure. Mary has Epilepsy. But, yes getting upset can bring them on."

"Does she have those things very often?"

"That is the only one I ever knew about. I was not even aware she was an Epileptic until her parents told me when they came to take her home"

"Can a person die from that?"

"Oh, I don't really know; I don't think so. Judy, the nurse, told me there are reliable medications that prevent it. The only problem is that people either neglect or forget to take their medication. But, sometimes, even when they are

Uncle Charlie Is A Rounder

taking the medication, a very stressful event might bring on a seizure."

"I bet that's what happened to Mary, 'cause she seems like a person who doesn't forget stuff."

"You're right Paul. Well, I have to get to work. I'll see you later."

"Okay. See ya Granny."

The very next week, Paul had to quit his job and go back home, because school would be starting soon. He had a great summer. He made more money than he ever dreamed he would. He had an experience of working on a major construction job. He learned about heavy equipment and was even given opportunities to operate several machines. He learned what it was to live on his own and away from home. He made friends that he would not soon forget. He also learned that a girl does not have to be a cupi doll to be desirable. He was grateful to his uncle in spite his being a rounder, because, after all, Uncle Charlie was responsible for Paul coming to Oklahoma City in the first place.

Paul had experienced his first love, his first kiss and his first heartache. He never again heard a word about Mary, but he would never forget her; and he will wonder about what ever happened to her for the rest of his life.

THE END

CHEROKEE WISDOM

CHEROKEE WISDOM

One evening an old Cherokee Indian was telling his grandson that every person has a struggle between two wolves taking place inside their bodies.

He said, "One of the wolves is called evil and the other one is called good."

He continued, "The evil wolf represents anger, envy, jealousy, sorrow, regret, greed, arrogance, self-pity, guilt, resentment, inferiority, lies, false-pride, superiority and ego."

"What does the other wolf represent, Grandpa?"

"The good wolf represents joy, peace, hope, serenity, humility, kindness, benevolence, empathy, generosity, truth, compassion, faith and love."

The boy asked, "If the two wolves get in a fight, which one wins?"

His Grandpa answered, "The one that gets fed."

LOST BEHIND ENEMY LINES

LOST BEHIND ENEMY LINES

During the winter of 1944. Nick Mueller was a Private First Class who was serving with a combat Signal Battalion somewhere in northeast Belgium during World War II. He and his squad leader were returning to their unit, after having gone back to a supply company to pick up some cases of K rations.

As they were driving along, on the road back, Nick opened some of the cases and began filling his pack and his squad leader's pack with as many boxes of K rations as they would hold. And, since he had long ago taken his gas mask and his extra clips of ammo from his own pack, it held a good supply of K's. Although Nick's squad was in a combat zone, his main duty was laying communication lines, so he seldom had his carbine with him; it too was in the back of a weapons carrier truck. The two soldiers were visiting as they drove along. It was a cloudy overcast day in the middle of December of 1944. The ground was covered with snow; the temperature was several degrees bellowing freezing.

Suddenly the Sgt. began to slow the jeep down as he approached a fork in the road. When he arrived at the fork, he stopped the Jeep and turned to Mule. That was the nickname Nick's squad had dubbed him.

Carl Otto

He leaned on the steering wheel for a moment before he said, "Mule, do you remember crossing this point on the way to that supply unit?"

Nick answered, "To tell the truth, I wasn't paying much attention to the road. I can't say one way or another."

The Sgt. sat without comment for another long moment, slowly shaking his head back and forth.

"No, we never came this way. We are on the wrong road."

He turned the Jeep engine off and raised his hand to indicate silence.

Nick was not yet nineteen years old and he was completely dependent on his Sgt.. He had absolutely no idea where they were. He was aware they were somewhere in Belgium, but since it was not his responsibility to be navigator, he had not paid much attention to the roads. As he saw the concerned look on his squad leader's face, he began to get a bit anxious.

"What are we going to do, Paul?"

"I think we will go back to that last intersection we crossed and see if we can remember anything about it."

He turned the Jeep around and went back in the direction from which they had come. Arriving at the intersection, he stopped again and they both looked around and tried to hear something. They could hear the distant sound of artillery in the direction Paul assumed to be north.

250

Lost Behind Enemy Lines

Paul remarked, "Nuts, I don't even have my compass; I left the dad gummed thing in the weapons carrier."

Nick said, "Well, you never really need it. Heck I don't even have my carbine with me."

"I'm going to pull over under that little grove of trees and we will just wait around a few minutes; maybe someone else will come by."

Then he slammed his fist on the steering wheel saying, "Son of a sea cook, if that ain't the dumbest darn thing I have ever done. We have been driving along here, shooting the breeze, and I don't know where in the heck we are."

Nick put in, "Surely someone else will show up before long."

"It would help if it wasn't so dad gummed cold. I'm glad we have our overcoats on. I don't know if it's the situation we're in or if it is actually getting colder."

Nick replied, "I think it is getting colder. What are we going do, drive all the way back to that supply unit?"

"Heck, I'm so dad gummed confused, I can't remember which one of these crooked roads we came on."

After a moment, he put the jeep in gear and headed down one of the curving roads. "I guess we'll give this one a shot. I don't even know what direction we're headed."

Mule answered, "I can't help you there; the only direction I know is straight up, and I'm not really sure of that."

Carl Otto

They didn't go very far before they topped a hill and Paul slammed on the brakes so hard he killed the engine. "Holy horse feathers! Look at that!"

Looking out over a valley, they could see what appeared to be more German tanks and trucks than you could count.

Nick said, "I don't think they can see us because of those trees behind us."

Paul started the jeep and slowly backed down over the crest of the hill. He turned around and headed back. He was mumbling to himself, "Holy horse feathers, I was hoping we had those Krauts pretty well whipped, but that mass of tanks makes things look a lot different."

Nick asked, "What are we going to do now?"

"We're getting our tails out of here."

Arriving back at the last intersection, they took another road that seemed to be heading into a more wooded area. After several miles of travel they could see a small village in the near distance. Paul pulled off the road and parked the jeep in an area of thick hedge-like brush. It was beginning to get late in the afternoon.

Paul said, "Grab your carbine and let's - -"

"Remember, I said I didn't bring my carbine."

"You don't have your Carbine! You little dummy. You should always have your carbine with you. And why in the heck didn't you pay more attention to the dad blamed roads?"

252

"Hey Sarge, knock it off. Don't go jumping my frame for something like this; you told me to leave my carbine in the truck. Good gravy, I'm not infantry anymore. That thing is in the way when I climbing a tree or a pole."

"Oh I know. You're right. I remember. I'm sorry; it's just that I screwed up, and I don't like screwing up. Let's leave the jeep here and walk over to that little village. We will take our packs."

So they put their packs on and cautiously approached the village. When they arrived at the sign, naming the place, Paul said, "My gosh, I think we're in Germany."

"How could we be in Germany? I thought we had to cross the Siegrfeid line to get there."

"All I know is the last town of any size I remember seeing the name of this place on a map had Aachen on it."

"Is Aachen in Germany?"

"Mule, I'm not sure of anything right now. I know one thing; if we are in Germany, we're not very far across the line."

"What are we going to do?"

"Quit asking me that, I'm thinking."

"Well, I'm scared. I'm cold and I want to know what we're going to do?"

"The first thing we're going to do is check this little village out; it looks like it's deserted. It's going to be dark before we know it, and we need to find a place to hide."

253

Carl Otto

Cautiously creeping along a hedge fence, they listened intently as they went from house to house through the streets and looked in several buildings before they determined the town had indeed been evacuated. So Paul decided they would get inside one of the abandoned houses. The inside of a house afforded them some protection from the cold, and provided a place to hole up for the night.

Once inside a house, they found an upstairs room that had a lot of old clothing and rags scattered around; there was even a feather mattress on the floor. They decided to pile the clothes and rags in a corner, lie down on the rags and cover up with the mattress.

As they were covering up with the mattress, Paul said, "Do you have any water in your canteen?"

"Yes, mine is almost full, but I think it is frozen solid."

"Mine is frozen too. Let's get them under the covers with us so they can thaw out from our body heat."

"How much body heat can an old man like you generate?"

"Old man! Why you little - - - I'm only thirty-one."

"That's an old man to me."

"Shut up and go to sleep."

Suddenly they were awakened by the sound of Tanks rolling. Paul shoved the mattress aside, jumped to his feet and looked out the window. Just as suddenly, he dropped to his stomach.

"Oh my God! I think they saw me."

Lost Behind Enemy Lines

"Is it those German tanks we saw yesterday?"

"Yes, it's tanks, trucks and foot soldiers and it looks like they are launching some kind of big offensive."

Paul slowly peeked out the window again. Dropping back down he said, "Oh nuts, Mule, they did see me and they are sending soldiers this way; they are almost to the house now."

"How many?"

"There were too many to count."

"Now what are we going to do?"

It was obvious Paul was deeply concerned.

"Oh nuts! Nuts! Nuts! There is no way we can get out of this mess."

Nick was like a stone statue as he waited for Paul to make a decision. After a moment, Paul placed his finger to his lips, indicating to be quiet.

Carl Otto

"They haven't seen you, so you get back under that mattress and keep still. I don't think we have many alternatives. They have us outmanned at least twenty to one, and all we have is my carbine. There is no way we can fight our way out of this mess; we would both be killed in a flash. I'm going to surrender. Maybe you can get back to the jeep and get back to our unit."

Nick was almost to a point of hysteria when Paul grabbed him by the shoulders, shook him and whispered, "Now you listen to me. This is an order. I have to give up because they have seen me and are coming in the house right now. There is no way we can get out of here. So, you take my carbine and both packs and keep still. I am taking this white rag and going down the stairs to meet them. I think I can convince them I am alone."

He then shoved Nick back in the corner, covered him with the rags and old clothes and then put the mattress over the top of him.

He whispered, "Just hold your breath and don't move if they come up here."

Paul then walked out of the room and down the stairs as he waved the white piece of clothing in front of himself. Nick could hear Paul telling the Germans he was alone, but one of them came upstairs, entered the room and even jerked the mattress partially away from the corner. But Nick held his breath and remained undetected under the rags.

256

Lost Behind Enemy Lines

He never moved a muscle until the sound of the last tank or truck had faded away.

Now he was alone behind enemy lines. Finally he pushed the clothes and mattress aside and slowly rose to his feet. He cautiously peeked out the window. It was almost totally dark but he could hear the sounds of German tanks and other vehicles on another road in the distance, but there seemed to be no sounds coming from the village. He cautiously went across the hall and tried to look out a window in the direction where he thought he could remember the jeep was hidden. Again he could hear more tanks and trucks; he assumed all of them seemed to be headed in the same direction'

He thought, "I wonder if they are retreating. Nah, they can't be retreating."

He said aloud to himself, "Oh Lord, Paul, I just know I could never get back to that jeep. Oh Lord, help me, what am I going to do? What am I gonna do?"

He began to realize how thirsty he was getting, so he felt his way back through the darkness to the corner, opened his canteen and took a long drink of the water that had thawed. Then he felt Paul had left his canteen. He had no alternatives; he would remain where he was for the rest of the night. He kept listening for vehicles, but he heard nothing but the sound of muffled movement in a distance until about mid morning of the next day when another convoy of trucks a

Carl Otto

approached from the same direction from which the first convoy came. The convoy went right through the middle of the little village and on out sight.

Nick thought, "Oh boy. The Krauts really are starting a big push somewhere, there goes another convoy on that road about a mile from here."

Nick was going over the instructions he had been given about what to do if he were ever captured. He said aloud, "I guess it's pretty simple. Just Name Rank and serial number; that's all; I think I can remember that. I hope Paul's captors were not mean to him."

As the day wore on the temperature seemed to continue to drop and more snow started falling. He crawled back under the mattress to get warm again, and before he went to sleep he was thinking, "It looks like there's going to be a white Christmas around here for sure."

When he awakened he could hear someone else in the room. The person was pulling at some of the clothing that was piled in the corner. Nick just froze for a moment. He held his breath as long as he could and them began breathing ever so slowly.

It seemed obvious, from the careful movements and heavy breathing of whoever was in the room, and the absence of any conversation, that it was only one person. So he slowly grasped the carbine and shoved the mattress aside, pointing the carbine toward the individual. There was a short gasp of quickly inhaled breath followed by the person just crumpling in a faint to floor in front of him.

Nick could readily see the person was a small civilian female. He was completely dumbfounded. He rose to his feet and went to the person where he could see it was a young girl no older than was he. He bent over and felt her hand; she was cold as ice. For some reason, Nick had no fear of this intruder; in fact, he was so glad it was not a German Soldier he was actually elated to see her. So he picked her up and placed her in the warm spot where he had just been, sat down on the floor next to her and pulled the mattress back up over both of them.

He was thinking as he pulled that feather mattress over them, "I never knew there was such a thing as a feather mattress, but boy they sure make a good cover."

The girl was regaining consciousness as he covered her. She started to rise and she looked as if she was going to scream, but he held his hands up and the put a finger to his lips. The girl quickly realized she was in a warm spot and that Nick was a young person who seemed to mean her no harm.

After a moment, in near perfect English, she said, "Are you American Soldier?"

"Yes. I am an American Soldier, and I will not harm you. Are you alone?"

"Yes, I am by myself alone."

Carl Otto

"What are you doing here in this town? It seems to be completely evacuated."

"I am lost. I was delivered to this town by some people who were going back to Central Germany. I thought I had relatives here."

"Did you find your relatives?"

She shook her head as she answered, "I had seen not a single person; not even a chicken or a dog or a cat, until yesterday when many German vehicles and soldiers passed near my hiding place."

"Are you hungry?"

"Yes, I am always hungry. I am very hungry. Do you have food?"

He never answered; he reached in one of the back backs and pulled out a package of K rations. He opened a can of potted meat and the package of four crackers. She wolfed them all down like it was the best meal she had ever eaten. Then he gave her the small chocolate candy bar and a drink from Paul's canteen.

As he watched her eat, he said, "You speak good English. Did you learn it in school?"

"My mother is language teacher. I have speak it since was I a little girl."

Nick could not help but notice how she savored that little chocolate bar.

"Tastes good, huh?"

260

Lost Behind Enemy Lines

She said, "I cannot now remember the last time I did eat chocolate."

Nick asked, "Are you sure there are no others here in this town, and that you are alone?"

"All others are away gone. I have been in a cellar hiding. But it is getting so cold. I reasoned I must find more clothing or blankets to keep me warm. That is reason I am here coming."

Then she asked, "But what are you alone here doing?"

"My squad leader and I got lost while going back to supply for more food."

He continued, "Did you see all the German tanks?"

"Yes, and I have a battery radio. I have listen also to events. Herr Hitler is making big offensive to go to sea and capture gasoline. Oh, I know not when he will be wise enough to surrender and make this War be ended."

Nick responded, "All I can say is that he will never defeat the Americans. So far, I think the cold weather is worse than the fighting."

"What do you intend for to do? Am I prisoner now? I think I want to be a prisoner because I am so alone and frightened."

Nick asked, "Are you German?"

"Yes, I am German, but I am not Nazi. Am I your prisoner?"

Carl Otto

Nick answered, "Well, to tell you the truth, I don't know whether you are my prisoner or I am your prisoner."

"But you are American Soldier and I am German citizen."

"Well, guess what? I am not a German citizen but I am German, though I do not speak the language. My grandparents on both sides of my family immigrated from Germany to Minnesota."

"What is your name?"

"Nick Meuller, but my buddies call me Mule."

She chuckled, "Is not a Mule a farm animal?"

"Yes, but Mule is just short for Meuller. What is your name?"

"I am named Katrina Lindelhaupt."

He was shocked as he answered, "Lindelhaupt! That is my mother's maiden name. Her grandparents came from Frankfort."

"Is this not a strange happening? My grandfather Lindelhaupt was raised in Frankfort, and for many years, while he was a young man, he lived in Chicago. He came back to Germany because my grandmother was here."

"Katrina, is this little town in Germany?"

"Yes, it is almost located upon the border from Belgium."

Suddenly they began to hear artillery and other noises of war.

262

Lost Behind Enemy Lines

Katrina said, "I think Herr Hitler's offensive must be getting closer to us."

Nick raised up. "Where is this cellar you have been hiding in?"

"It is underneath a house that has been badly damaged."

"Is it in a pretty isolated spot?"

"Yes. It is a much safer place than in this present room."

"Good. Let's gather up as much of this stuff as we can carry and go to that cellar. If the coast is clear, I will come back and get this mattress too."

"Does this mean I am now your prisoner?"

"Oh, what the heck; yes, I guess you are my prisoner."

She replied, "That is good; I am so alone frightened."

So the two of them began looking through the clothing and rags on the floor. Katrina had found a pair of men's trousers she could wear, a large sweater she could put on over her other clothing and a man's overcoat with the sleeves gone. She put them all on.

Nick noticed her shoes were definitely not the kind to afford any protection in this weather, so he said, "Sit down here. I am going to tie some of these rags around your feet, over your shoes."

He bundled her feet up with several garments and then ripped some rags into strips to tie the rags to her feet.

Carl Otto

She was saying, as she watched him work, "Oh, this is great idea. My feet were so cold, and I am beginning already to feel the warmth."

He also found a large wool shirt, tore the sleeves of it and pulled them up over his own boots. They then gathered together the two back packs and canteens, a big bundle of rags and Paul's carbine and headed for the cellar. Luckily there were no soldiers anywhere near this small village. So after they had all the stuff in the cellar, he started back to get the mattress.

Katrina grasped his arm and asked, "You are not preparing to leave me alone, are you?"

"No, I am not preparing to leave you; I might need you more than you need me. I'll be back. I'm going to get that feather mattress."

Arriving back at the cellar, he found Katrina eating another box of K rations.

She said, "Oh my goodness, these boxes of food are good; especially the little chocolate candy."

"Yes, they are not bad, and those crackers have all the vitamins and minerals we need too."

"She continued, "And, I find there is placed in each box, a small package of four cigarettes. Do you smoke them?"

"No. I don't smoke; I just give mine to other soldiers who do."

Lost Behind Enemy Lines

She said, "Did you know these cigarettes can for money be used."

"What do you mean?"

"I am saying, some people will give most anything they own for American Cigarettes."

"How about that? I'll tell you what we'll do. As we eat the K rations, we will start putting the little packets of cigarettes in the empty boxes. When we get out of here, you can keep all of them an use them for money."

"Oh I could not do that."

"Nonsense, if I can get back to the jeep, there are more cases of K rations. We will have a lot of buying power."

"What is Jeep?"

"A jeep is a small army vehicle."

"You mean like automobile?"

"Yes, it is an army automobile."

"And you one of this jeep have?"

"Yes, my squad leader parked the jeep in a bunch of bushes and we walked to this little town. Then when the Germans came through here, they saw Paul looking out the window and started coming to get us. He decided it was best for him to surrender. He ordered me to stay and try to get back to our squad later."

"Oh my goodness, he must be an excellent gentleman."

"He really is. I hope he is being treated okay."

"What is he named?"

265

Carl Otto

"Paul Lockner; he is also of German descent."

"If he is not Jewish, he will be treated humanly."

"He's not Jewish, but I am still worried about him."

The afternoon was fading away and it would not be long before darkness began to creep in. Nick decided there probably would not be a better time to go back to the jeep and get some more K rations. He told Katrina he remembered the fencerow he and Paul had crouched against as they made their way to the village, so he was confident he could go to the jeep and be back before total darkness was upon them.

She said, "Perhaps I should along also go. I can help with carry things."

He thought a moment before he answered, "Okay. We haven't seen any sign of anyone; I think you're right. We can bring back more stuff."

So the two of them set out along the fence. It did not take long before they arrived at the jeep. Nick started to unload some cases of K rations. Then he discovered an empty duffle bag folded up and placed under the driver's seat.

"Oh, Great! I will break these cases open and fill this duffle bag; we can carry a lot more that way. You flatten the empty case boxes and push them under the jeep."

While opening boxes and filling the duffle bag, he also found a barracks bag with some tools in it. He dumped the tools and filled the barracks bag. Then he grabbed a flashlight from the toolbox and they started back toward the cel-

Lost Behind Enemy Lines

lar. The snow was falling heavily again and the wind was picking up.

Nick said, "In a way this snow and wind might be a good thing for us, because of two things; one, we can drag these bags across the snow easier than we can carry them, and, two; the drifting snow is covering our tracks."

It was totally dark by the time they had the two bags of K rations down in the cellar. Luckily, the cellar had a fairly tight door to the outside and also an entrance inside the demolished house; it was an excellent hiding place.

Nick unloaded the bags and, in the light from the flashlight, Katrina began stacking the rations on some shelves on the wall. Nick suggested they put some of the boxes under the bedding on which they slept; that way their body heat would thaw the frozen cans. He then looked out the door and noticed the moon was peeking out of the cloud cover.

He said, "The moon is coming out, so I can see well enough to go back to that room and get some more rags for bedding."

He took the duffle bag and told Katrina, "You sit tight while I'm gone. I won't be long."

"What is this 'sit tight?'"

"It's just an expression that means stay here."

Again she wanted to go along, but he told her the one duffle bag should hold all the stuff that was there. He also told her to listen to her radio and see if she could hear any

267

Carl Otto

news. However, when she tried her radio, she discovered the battery had gotten so weak she could not pick up a station.

Nick made the trip within less than twenty minutes. They piled the clothes in a corner and, in the pitch-black darkness of the cellar they again pulled the feather mattress over them as a cover. Nick had decided they should use the flashlight very sparingly, because he had no more batteries.

After a long moment of pitch-black silence, Katrina said, "I am so happy you were in that house. I was so frightened and hungry and cold. Now I am have full belly. I am warm and I and no so much frightened. And my feet are much warmed also."

He never answered. He just reached his arm out and put it on her shoulder. As he did, she scooted close to him and he hugged her with both arms as she snuggled close.

"Oh my Katrina, I am so happy it was you who came up to that room. I don't know what is going to happen to us. Maybe if the German army finds us first, you can help save me; I know if the Americans find us first, I can save you. We will just take one hour at a time, but for now, let's get some sleep."

It was not long before their combined body heat, under the excellent insulation of that feather mattress had them both warm and comfortable; they slept well.

When Nick awakened he discovered Katrina was not there. He reached for the flashlight and began looking

Lost Behind Enemy Lines

around the cellar. Suddenly the cellar door came open and someone scrambled down the steps. Nick turned the flashlight off but he soon realized it was Katrina coming down the steps.

He said, "What in the world have you been doing outside?"

Through chattering teeth, she answered, "When I this morning woke up, I was so warm I was to nearly perspiring. My warm body stench was so much bad I could not myself stand to smell. So, I went outside and a snow bath took."

"Oh for God's sake, you were concerned about your body odor? You could freeze to death before you realized anything in this cold. Get under these covers right now."

So she immediately crawled under the feather mattress with Nick and he held her close. She was shaking and her teeth were chattering.

While Katrina was getting warmed up again, Nick asked, "How old are you?"

"My age will turn sixteen years on January 5. I suppose your age to be much the same as me."

"Yes, as you say it, my age will turn nineteen on February 10."

He continued, "Do you have a family? And if you do, do you know where they are?"

"My father was forced to be in the Army when he was forty-eight year old already. The last I hear about him, he

Carl Otto

was in North Africa somewhere. I did a brother have who was twenty-two when the SS Nazi's did shoot him to death because they did say he was English spy. Perhaps it was due to his attending a school in England when he was ten years old. And he did learn to speak with British sound."

"That's terrible. What about your mother?"

"I was never to find out where my mother was sent. I was in a youth camp placed when I was ten, and while in that camp they told me I had to have appendix removed. I was not even sick a little bit. At age twelve, I learned that all girls in the camp who did not blue eyes have or light hair have, were taken to infirmary to have appendix removed. I know at this time that they did more than appendix remove, because I have never any periods started."

Nick was pretty naïve, and he was not sure what she meant, but his speculation was correct.

"Those rotten rats. Paul told me about how Hitler had set up whole towns where only blonde blue eyed physically superior men and women lived, and that they were to have as many kids as possible. And, that they actually sterilized people they thought were inferior."

She added, "It is true, because I did some blond and blue eye friends have who, when they turned seventeen, were selected to be married to men they did not even know. Herr Hitler said he would a master race develop to rule the world."

270

Lost Behind Enemy Lines

Nick responded, "Well, from the looks of all the tanks and other military wheels we have been seeing roll, Herr Hitler has more power than we have suspected."

They sat for a moment without talking further before Katrina asked if she could have another box of food.

"Of course. Here, I put several boxes under where we have been sleeping so they would be a bit warmer from our body heat. You eat one any time you feel the need."

"That was excellent idea. I am again quite hungry."

So they opened two more K ration boxes and had breakfast. Water was not a problem because there was plenty of snow available.

Nick's mind was in a complete quandary. He was frightened and unsure what his next move would be. He realized he was in as safe of hiding place as possible for the time being; no one would know the location of the cellar in which they were hiding, unless they knew in advance or just stumbled upon it. He realized the weather outside was so bitter cold that it was unwise to try to do much of anything, yet he kept thinking about what Paul had said about him getting back to the jeep and trying to return to the outfit.

At least he was secure in the knowledge he was not alone. He had this little stranger with him, and somehow he felt responsible for keeping her safe.

Carl Otto

Suddenly a thought entered his mind, "I wonder if that jeep battery would operate her radio. If it would we might be able to learn what was going on."

He said, "Katrina, as soon as we finish eating breakfast, we are going to take that little battery radio of yours to the jeep and see if your batteries might be recharged."

He slowly opened the cellar door and peeked out. He listened intently and could hear nothing except the sound of distant artillery. So he opened the door, stood up and looked around.

Since they were in an area that was like a no-man's land. There was not a sound or sight of anything close.

They didn't have to bundle up; they already were wearing all the clothes they had on their backs. They took the radio and the empty duffle bag and headed for the jeep. When they arrived at their destination, they discovered the jeep and the brush area nearly drifted over with snow.

Nick worked his way around to the front and unhooked the hood latches. He raised the hood, removed the small square battery from the radio, removed two sparkplug wires from the jeep and placed the radio battery between the jeep battery terminals. Using the two sparkplug wires he made contacts with the radio battery.

There were sparks when he touched one of the wires from the positive pole on the jeep battery to the pole on the

Lost Behind Enemy Lines

radio battery. He held the wires in place for several minutes before he put the battery back in the radio.

His experiment worked. The radio began picking up several radio stations.

"Holy smoke, I can't believe we had such luck; it works."

"What is this holy smoke?"

"It's just a slang expression."

Suddenly a crisp British voice came on the radio, "—the fighting is very heavy in and around Bastogne. The many Panzer units that have been involved in this winter offensive seem to have been stopped. The loss of lives has been heavy on both sides; however, it seems the Allied forces are beginning to prevail, and this last big push may be the beginning of the end of this war."

He turned the radio off and said, "Okay, let's load this duffle bag with more K rations and get back to the cellar."

They were able to get all of the remaining K rations into the duffle bag. They headed back to the cellar. By the time they arrived back in the cellar, Katrina was shaking from the cold. The two youngsters huddled down under the feather mattress. She was curled up with her back against Nicks belly and chest and he was holding her tight. They were both shivering.

He said, "Oh boy, I wonder just how cold it is out there. I'll bet it must be at least ten below zero."

273

Carl Otto

After several minutes they were warm enough that they no longer shivered.

Nick said, "Well, Little Buddy, at least we are getting warm and we're not hungry."

She giggled as she responded, "I guess if I am 'Little Buddy,' you must be, 'Big Buddy.'"

She continued, "Nick, I have now my back nice and warm, may I now my belly also get warm."

He chuckled, "Sure you can. Roll over, and now you can your belly also get warm. It tickles me the way you sometimes scramble your words."

"I know. My pronounce is good, but, as you say, my scramble is also good."

She lay with her head against Nick's chest for a moment before she turned her face upward and asked, "Do you have wife or girl in America?"

He laughed as he answered, "No, I don't have a wife. I was dating a girl when I left home, but in the last letter I received, while I was in England, she told me it was okay for me to go out with other girls. I assumed from that, that she was dating other guys."

"So you are not thinking about going home to her when this war is over."

"No, as a matter of fact, she is the last thing I have been thinking about. I have been thinking about how to keep

274

Lost Behind Enemy Lines

from freezing to death, how to keep from being shot or captured and what to do with you"

"Am I not help to keep you from freezing? And, if the German army finds us, I will help from you getting not shot?"

"Yes, you are a big help." He hugged her tighter.

She spoke no more for a long moment as they just held on to each other.

Finally, she looked back up and said, "Nick, right now I have no other feeling than to be warm and to be needed. It is not time for anything else, but it is time for me to something do for a boy that I have never done."

"Oh? And what is that?"

"I have by a boy never been kissed. Will you kiss me?"

He smiled as he took her face in his two hands. He looked into her face for a short moment and then he put his lips against hers. He held the kiss for a long moment before he released her.

"Thank you Katrina for letting me to be the first boy to kiss you. I liked it very much."

"I liked it very much too. And, you may again kiss me as the wish to do so comes to your mind."

Again he chuckled as he pulled her more tightly against his body.

He was thinking, "Oh my Lord. In my wildest dreams, I would never have guessed I would find myself in this position. Here I am, lost behind the lines, in a war that I had

Carl Otto

nothing to do with starting. I'm scared I'll never get out of it alive, I am worried about my friend, Paul, yet I cannot abandon the hope that things will turn out okay. I am hiding in a cellar under the rubbish of a destroyed house, in a foreign land, and I have this little warm body cuddled against me, and somehow she seems to give me the strength to hold on."

Katrina was quiet and Nick was quiet. The two of them remained under the warmth of that big old feather mattress. They both fell into a deep sleep.

These two young people had the security of a cellar in an abandoned town; they had the security of a supply of K rations; there was plenty of clean snow for drinking water and they had each other, but they also lived with the fear that all this could be gone in the blink of an eye.

Nick was shouldered with the responsibility of making all the decisions because all Katrina had known her entire life was an existence in which others made all the decisions; however, her existence with Nick was so vastly different and she trusted him so implicitly that her fears seemed to wane in his presence. He was worried, but she was confident he would find a way to save them both.

Days went on and Nick had made a decision. One late afternoon he said to Katrina, "Tomorrow, I am going to go see if I can get that jeep started and out of that snow drift.

Lost Behind Enemy Lines

We have only a few days supply of food, so something has to be done."

"You're not going to leave me alone here, are you?"

"No, I am not going to leave you. I am going to keep you with me as long as I can."

"Nick do you believe in God?"

"Well, it's kind of hard to believe in much of anything when you find yourself in a mess like this. What about you? Do you believe in God?"

"Yes I do, and I say a prayer every night before I go to sleep."

"Are you praying that God will take us out of here and make this war end."

"Oh, yes I do. Tonight I would like for you to with me pray. Perhaps if we together pray, God will hear us."

"Well, Little Buddy, it couldn't hurt anything. So, tonight I will pray with you."

That night when they settled in under the feather bed, Katrina put her hands on Nick's face and said, "Are you ready for to pray with me."

"Sure. You say what you want and I will repeat after you."

"Okay. Shut your eyes and after me repeat."

"Go ahead."

"Dear God."

"Dear God."

Carl Otto

"Please to listen to my words."

"Please to listen to my words."

"If it is in your power."

"If it is in your power."

"Will you please help for to save me and my new companion."

"Well you please help save me and my new companion."

"From this terrible war."

"From this terrible war."

"Amen."

Nick added, "And Lord, I thank you for bringing Katrina to me. I promise I will do everything in my power to keep her safe. Amen."

Once again they huddled close and held each other tightly as they drifted off to sleep.

Nick was awakened from his sound sleep as Katrina was shaking him and whispering.

"I hear the sound of machines running."

Nick jumped to his feet, went up the steps to the cellar door and raised it very slowly about an inch. He could see a half-track, loaded with German soldiers, on the street not far from his position. Close behind the half-track were several trucks; also loaded with German soldiers.

Within minutes, the ground was shaking as many tanks and trucks were rolling through the streets of the little town

Lost Behind Enemy Lines

in the direction from which they had first come when Paul was captured.

He turned to Katrina, "I think they are retreating."

Suddenly there was a roar of airplanes overhead, followed by a loud explosion. The first wave of planes was followed by more airplanes and many more explosions; the war had definitely come to their little hideaway.

Katrina asked, "What are we going to do?"

"We're going to get back under that featherbed and keep still. I just hope none of those bombs hit this house."

The sounds of the moving vehicles seemed to be fading away and there were no more airplane sounds. They could hear some sounds of people groaning. Nick assumed the airplanes were Allied planes, and they had been bombing and strafing retreating German troops.

Nick felt around under the clothing for the carbine. He took the carbine and went to the top of the stairs, where he once again slowly raised the door.

Suddenly, without warning, someone opened the cellar door. Nick was standing face to face with an enemy soldier. The German pointed his rifle toward Nick, and Nick fired his weapon at close range right into the middle of the man's chest. The man fell backwards without so much as a sound.

That was the first time Nick had fired a weapon since basic training, and he had just killed a man.

Carl Otto

When the dead soldier fell backwards, he released his hold on the cellar door and it fell wide open. Nick kept his head down as low as possible, but he could not reach the opened door without exposing himself further. The next thing he knew, another German soldier was standing at the cellar opening with a gun pointing at him; this time the man fired a shot into the cellar before Nick killed him.

He turned to Katrina, "Are you okay?"

"Yes, the bullet did not come my way."

Nick started to step back in the cellar, but as he did, a potato masher grenade was tossed down the steps. Luckily Nick caught it in mid air and threw it back out of the cellar; it exploded within seconds after he tossed it back out of the cellar.

He poised himself for another grenade, but there were no more. He waited a few minutes and could hear no more movement, so he cautiously peeked out of the cellar.

Five dead German soldiers were within ten feet of the cellar opening and the snow was covered with blood, but there seemed to be no more soldiers around.

Nick could hear vehicles at a distance, and he could hear artillery and small arms fire, but none of it seemed to be in the little village. He reached up and pulled the cellar door closed again. Then he went back down to Katrina. She was crying, but somehow Nick felt like everything was going to be okay.

Lost Behind Enemy Lines

He said, "Come here to me. Lets sit back down and cover up again. My heart is beating like it was going to pound through my chest, but I don't think there are any more soldier out there."

She cuddled up close to Nick as they sat and pulled the mattress up to their chins. He had the carbine pointed toward the cellar door.

Another hour passed before the heard any more sounds. This time the sounds were being made be American Soldiers as squads of foot soldiers started coming into view.

Nick pushed the cellar door back open and told Katrina to find something white that he could tie on the barrel of the carbine. She handed him a lady's blouse and he fastened it to the gun barrel. He reached as high as he could with the carbine and waved it back and forth.

He heard, "Hey Sarge, there is someone trying to surrender."

Nick yelled, "I am an American Soldier."

The guy yelled back, "The hell you are. Who won the World Series in 1938?"

Nick was puzzled. He hesitated before he called back, "I don't know who won the 1938 World Series. What's that got to do with me?"

By then there were several American soldiers within a few yards of the cellar opening.

281

Carl Otto

One of them called, "What is your name rank and serial number?"

By then, Nick was getting a bit agitated. He just tossed the carbine out on the ground and walked up the steps of the cellar.

"I am Pfc. Nick Mueller; I am attached to the 49th Combat Signal Battalion; my squad leader is Paul Lockner and he was captured about a month ago."

"Okay, kid. Is there anyone else down there with you?"

"Yes, there is a German girl, but she is not a Nazi. She is with me, and I am keeping her with me."

Suddenly an officer appeared in a jeep. The Sgt talked to the captain for a moment and then he told Nick and Katrina to go over to the captain's jeep.

They walked to the jeep and Nick saluted the captain. The captain's jeep was totally enclosed and was fitted with a heater. He told them to get in; he was taking them back to an aid station.

By the time they were in the jeep, both Nick and Katrina were shivering from the cold. The captain's driver turned the heater to its highest setting and turned the fan on full blast. They sat huddled in the back seat and the captain and his driver sat in front.

On the road back to the aid station, Nick related the complete story of how he happened to be behind the lines, and how Katrina and he happened to be together.

282

Lost Behind Enemy Lines

The capt. Asked, "What about those five dead krauts outside that cellar where you were?"

He answered, "I shot two of them with Paul's carbine, and I caught a potato masher they tossed in the cellar and threw it back out. I guess it killed the other three."

The driver said, "You're telling us you tossed a potato masher back out of that cellar."

"Yes Sir, I was real lucky, 'cause when it was tossed in, it landed right in my hands; I just gave it a quick toss back out before it went off."

The Capt. said, "You say you had Paul's carbine. Where was your own rifle?"

"Well, that's a long story, Capt. You see, I'm a pole climber so most of the time my rifle is in the truck. It was there the day Paul and I got lost."

Suddenly the captain said, "Wait a minute. You said you name is Mueller and your Sgt. is named Lockner. When I stop to think, I remember when we had that prisoner exchange, there was a Sgt. with a German name who said he had left a kid he called 'Mule,' when he surrendered, in a house in some small village - - - - -"

Nick shouted, "Yee Hah, Paul got liberated. I'm Mule, that's what he calls me because my name is Mueller. Is he okay?"

Nick was so overcome with joy he started weeping.

283

Carl Otto

Katrina hugged him and said, "I am so happy for you, that your friend is okay."

Nick was jubilant for the moment, but when they reached the aid station he did not anticipate what would take place. The captain had his driver pull to a stop in front of a building, and Katrina was told to get out and go with two MP's.

Nick said, "Wait a minute Sir. Why is she taken away from me? What are they going to do with her?"

The captain turned and said, "Son. You are in the army and this girl is now being placed under supervision until we decide what to do with her."

"But, Sir. She is not an enemy. I could not have survived without her. Please don't separate us like this."

The captain was thoughtful for a moment before he answered.

"Private Mueller, I am going to bend the rules a little here. I am going to allow you to go in the building with this girl. I will instruct them to allow the two of you to be alone for an hour. In that time you should be able to exchange and record all the information you need about one another. Then when the war is over, you will be on your own to find each other again, if you so wish."

"Do you mean, Sir, that one hour is all we have?"

"I'm sorry Son, but I shouldn't even be allowing one minute. My driver will be back to pick you up in an hour."

Lost Behind Enemy Lines

The two of them were then taken to a small room, given some writing paper and pencils, and left alone.

Nick and Katrina held each other and she cried.

Nick was having difficulty keeping his composure.

"We don't have much time right now, so let's write the names and addresses of all our people we know of on paper. When this war is over, we will find each other."

Nick had several addresses and even telephone numbers on his list, but Katrina had so little to go on.

She said, "All I know is that I once had family in Frankfort. So when this war is all over, I will go to Frankfort to live. And each Sunday I will go to the Big Railway Station where I will try to be present at the bronze statue of the horseman that stands in the front of the building. I will be there each Sunday from 1 pm until 2 pm. And I will write letters to the addresses you have me given."

Exactly one hour after the door was closed on that little room, the two MP's were there to open it and take Katrina away.

Nick walked slowly out the door where the captain and his driver were waiting. It took three more days before Nick was once again reunited with his former unit. It was a grand reunion, and Nick was so happy to see his old friends, especially Paul.

The war in Europe was over within a few months of Nick's reunion with Paul, and their Battalion was transferred

Carl Otto

back to France where they were told they would be a part of the invasion of Japan. However, the atomic bomb changed the picture. Suddenly Japan had surrendered and the entire conflict was history. Paul had accumulated enough points that he was eligible for discharge, so he went home.

Nick, being one of the youngest members of the unit, did not have enough points to be eligible for discharge, so he was sent back to Germany in the Army of Occupation.

As fate would have it, he was stationed in Frankfort; he was jubilant when he found his new assignment was where Katrina said she would be. So, each Sunday afternoon, from 1pm until 2pm, it was Nick who showed up at the bronze statue of a horseman.

Nick was also receiving regular letters from the girl he had dated before he went overseas. And he did remember her with much fondness, but he could not erase the image of that skinny, ragged, dirty little Katrina from his mind.

As time went on, he began to miss a Sunday at the statue occasionally. Then he cut the time he remained at the statue from 1:50 pm until 2:05 pm. His one-year deployment with the Occupation force was almost at an end, and he had been placed on the schedule to be returned to the United States.

Nick decided to make one more stop at the statue. He caught a streetcar that made a stop within one block of the railway station. As he stepped off the streetcar and looked toward that Bronze Horseman, he saw a small figure leaning

Lost Behind Enemy Lines

on the wrought iron fence that surrounded the statue. The individual's back was turned in his direction, but he knew it had to be Katrina.

He walked slowly and deliberately toward her.

He was within twenty feet of Katrina when she seemed to sense he was there. She straightened her head and shoulders upward and made a quick turn around.

Neither of them said a word as Nick opened his arms and she ran to him. He grabbed her, lifted her tiny body off the ground and whirled around and around with he legs flying outward. Then he let her feet down and they simply held each other tightly and cried tears of joy.

Finally Nick broke the silence. "I had given up ever seeing you again. How long have you been in Frankfort?"

"I just arrived here today. In fact I got off the train less than one hour ago. How long have you been here?"

Nick answered, "Fate is so strange. You arrived here less than an hour ago, and I am scheduled to leave Frankfort at 0500 in the morning. Did you ever try to contact any of the people on the list I gave you?"

"I was unable to retain the list. I first tried to memorize it, but it was too extensive. Within one day of our parting, someone took the list from me, and I never knew who or why. I just never saw it again."

"Where have you been?"

"I was for a few weeks in a detention facility, and then

Carl Otto

I was sent to Munich where a job was awaiting me. I have been working there ever since."

She hesitated as if she had something more to say.

Nick asked, "Is there something you want to tell me."

"I don't know how to say this Nick, because the last thing in this world I would ever want to do, is hurt you."

"Are you trying to tell me you have a boyfriend?"

"I did not intend for it to happen - — "

"Katrina, it is all right. I am happy for you."

"I think you are telling me you have renewed your feelings for the girl you left in the United States."

He answered, "I have really been in a pickle. I have so wanted to see you again and know you are okay. I knew I had to tell you about Agnes, and the last thing in this world I would ever want to do is hurt you in any way."

He continued, "We spent some real special time together and I will never forget you as long as I live. We lived through a tragic part of our lives and were a great support for each other, and I love you in a special way I will never again love anyone."

She was looking intently into his eyes as she said, "I know what you are feeling, because I too will always love you and never forget you as long as I live. But our love is not the kind of love we should have for a life-long mate. I have found that love in another man and I think you have found it in your girlfriend."

Lost Behind Enemy Lines

"Yes, I have Katrina, and I can hardly wait to get home to her. She knows about you. I have told her everything. And, now I have more to tell her."

Katrina said, "Do you think we should continue to try to contact each other?"

"I think it would probably be better to leave things as they now are."

"You are right Nick. Let us not complicate the lives of our chosen mates with ghosts."

Carl Otto

Nick gathered he into his arms again and held her close for a long moment. That is all he wanted to do, because he knew they would never hold each other again.

Nick's last words to Katrina were, "For the rest of my life, I will always know I had the greatest little feather mattress buddy any human could ever have."

"Yes, Big Feather Mattress Buddy, we had a scary and uncertain time together, but we survived. May God always be with you."

They walked, arm in arm, to the streetcar stop where Katrina boarded a car headed east and Nick stood watching the car fade from his sight. The lump in his throat felt like it was as big as his fist as he slowly turned and walked toward another streetcar stop.

He thought, "I never dreamed this would turn out as it has. I had given up ever seeing her again, and now I have just given her up forever. Oh Lord, have I done the right thing? I have missed her so much; I love her with all my heart. But I know I had to let her go."

He boarded the next streetcar and seated himself in a seat next to an elderly lady. The car rolled along; clikity click, clickity click, clickity click.

Nick turned to the old lady and said, "She was right. We couldn't complicate our lives with ghosts."

Lost Behind Enemy Lines

The old lady looked at Nick and never answered as the car continued its steady, clickity click - clickity click - clickity click

THE END

EPILOGUE

I remember my dad telling about an old man who was always complaining to his wife that the coffee was too hot.

He would say, "Dad blast it, Old Woman. You always give me my cup of coffee while it is still boiling. There I went and burned the hair off my tongue again."

One day one of his grandsons was at the breakfast table when he made his complaint.

His grandson said, "Pour it out in yer sasser, Grandpap; that's what it's fer."

So I guess if "Grandpap" had been drinking it from his saucer, he wouldn't have burned his tongue.